Picture Theory

Prose Series 7

Nicole Brossard

Picture Theory

Translated from the French by
Barbara Godard

Guernica

Montreal, 1991

Original title:
Picture Theory

Picture Theory was first published in 1982 by Éditions Nouvelle Optique
and a revised edition was published in 1989 by Éditions de l'Hexagone.

Antonio D'Alfonso, publisher and editor.
Guernica Editions Inc.
P.O. Box 633, Station N.D.G.
Montreal (Quebec), Canada H4A 3R1

The Publisher and the Translator gratefully acknowledge the financial
support from The Canada Council and
Le ministère des Affaires culturelles du Québec.

Legal Deposit — 3rd Quarter.
Bibliothèque nationale du Québec and National Library of Canada.

Canadian Cataloguing in Publication Data
Brossard, Nicole, 1943–
[Picture theory. English]
Picture theory
(Prose series ; 7)
Translation of: Picture theory.
ISBN 0-920717-2205
I. Godard, Barbara II. Title. III. Title:
Picture theory. English. IV. Series.

PS8503.R7P5213 1991 C843'.54 C91-090295-X
PQ3919.2.B76P5213 1991

Contents

For Marisa Zavalloni

Preface

This is a book of light, of clair-voyance, about perception and the wave interaction of light through which is realized the virtuality of writing: 'Today a white light made them real.' Holography, or writing, is transformed in the whiteout of the scene of production/seduction where desire, time, memory 'flow as information in optical fibres', into the Hologram, a combinatory through which a potential woman is modelled: 'At the ultimate equation, I would loom into view.' '...she had come to the point in full fiction abundant(ly) to re/cite herself perfectly readable.' This is a move into abstraction, into specular fiction in the future anterior by a character/writer who will never be able to narrate, to make casual connections, but only to recombine signs in endlessly variable sets that generate varying pictures.

Picture Theory is a rewriting of the great modernist books of the night. 'Patriarchal machine for making the blues.' The Bloomsday of Joyce's nocturnal epic is transformed in the transparency of the amorous white scene of May 16th. Djuna Barnes' *Nightwood* is traversed by a golden helmeted woman, Claire Dérive, who, as clarity and transparency, 'the wave, the space, the memory', changes the angle of vision, sets adrift an abundance of vital abstractions to illuminate *Lightwood* with an Utopian impulse. Pursuing Gertrude Stein's cubist investigation of predicative logic and 'sentences', Brossard connects through the metonymic chain 'Stein' to the 'Picture Theory' of Wittgenstein with its propositional logic, its concern with the rules of syntax that discriminate sense and nonsense, its statement that a picture or model itself is a fact.

Brossard's project is a radical one, nothing less than to challenge the foundations of Aristotelian logic of binary oppositions on which are grounded theories of the sign, identity and representation, that fix 'woman' in discourse as lack or token of exchange. In this science fiction, which is also a fiction of science, an exploration of model theory, Brossard draws on the logics of becoming of post-relativity physics to postulate an interaction model of a subject in transformation which entails a theory of fiction as staged re-presentation, as the rearrangement of signifiers whose meanings are provisional, conditional. Fictional. Under the currently dominant discourse, fiction, imag(in)ing is the only possible way to effect new boundaries for the 'real', to postulate new (f)acts or pictures of exchanges between women in the plural. 'Were this text not lesbian it would make no sense,' wrote Brossard in *L'Amèr (These Our Mothers)*. In *Picture Theory,* she continues this project to elaborate possibilities for the exploded subject in a theory of lesbian textuality.

As text, *Picture Theory* develops a narrative that functions as hologram through a combinatory in which each unit is constantly redeveloped in new combinations. Through this process, virtual woman becomes actualized in the future as hologram. The mathematical models for the neighbourhood interactions of waves in the hologram are found in a series of transformational functions which like the differential equation of calculus involve a mathematical curve joining an infinity of discrete points in a passage toward a limit it never reaches. This is the operation of folding, an unfolding to infinity. But it is also an infolding of infinity: each segment of the curve contains, in potentiality, an infinite number of other functions and each point on the curve is divisible into an infinity of other points — each of which in turn belongs to yet another infinite set of potential functions, discrete elements linked in an endless curve. Brossard's text both thematizes the curve and light and enacts this folding in its writing, as phonemes, words (its discrete elements) are linked in many sets (networks) of infinite possible functions.

The problem for the translator is the problem for any reader, the problem of memory which the text enacts. Memory as wave interaction, as recombination, as flow. Reading engages the transformative work of memory. The reader must keep in mind the precise words through all their textual displacements and consequent drifts in meaning. In the absence of narrative connections holding the text together, or of leitmotifs, *Picture Theory* is linked by networks of signifiers. The translator must remember what combination she used previously for the same sets of phonemes and confront the complexities of change in semantic field necessitated by the different nuances in register of meaning in the French term and the English translated term. As a theory of sign activity as combinatory, of the text as paragram, in Julia Kristeva's terms, *Picture Theory* foregrounds a theory of the signifier as continuous difference, of a network of sliding signs which entails a theory of the transformativity of the translation effect. This theory is developed in the network of *dérive*, which is simultaneously the surrealist associative 'drift' of the sign, linguistic 'derivation' productive of language change and the mathematical function, the 'derivative'. Characters and issues are derived from the Steins — Gertrude and Ludwig — but set adrift on the play of the signifier.

My pursuit of the elusive sign to fix it, temporarily, in a translation of the text into English produced a desire for the revenge of narrative, a quest narrative for the veiled meaning of Brossard's text, a narrative in which the transferential process of the translation is enacted as the reading subject becomes the writing subject, a subject con-figured in/by the encounter with the textual object. I have written the fragmentary narrative of that process of epistemological transformation elsewhere in 'Essay/ons traduction/translation: The subject in/of translation.' Fragments from this dealing with technical issues of the translation of *Picture Theory* may be found in 'Re/Configurations' in *Raddle Moon* (Spring 1991). Here, it is important to signal to the reader how to approach the bilingualism of this text which moves across continents, across times, across languages in its efforts to destabilize identity and meaning. The meaning of English in a Quebec text and of French in an English text differ greatly in light of the politics of language in Canada where English is the language of the colonizer, the language of power. Consequently, in this translation, I have indicated the passages Brossard wrote in English in boldface. I have followed her practice of breaking with a unified language by putting passages into French without italics. Nonetheless I have been careful to choose sections where the French words are generally familiar to English-speaking readers so that the effect of drawing attention to the material signifier will not result in permanent puzzlement.

This has been an exciting text to translate and has posed challenges not only to my cognitive capacities but to my writing skills. I should like to thank several friends and colleagues for their help editing the translation, Gerry Shikatani and Lola Lemire Tostevin for their help with linebreaks in the 'poetic' sections, Ray Ellenwood for his sharp ear as we read 'prose' sections aloud together checking for missing words and phrases and rapid shifts in verb tenses. Though it bears the same title, this English version differs greatly from the French version of *Picture Theory*. With their help, however, its work on language, its status as text enters yet another network of signifiers to extend its productivity.

Barbara Godard

Repetition, a rehearsal without a spectacle makes no sense unless it is language (in) itself.

What can be said can only be said by means of a sentence, and so nothing that is necessary for the understanding of all sentences can be said.

Ludwig Wittgenstein

Now what is the difference between a sentence and I mean. The difference is the sentence is that they will wish women.

Gertrude Stein

THE ORDINARY

Chapter 1

▼

I exercise my faculty of synthesis here because again I must proceed with precision among sounds, bodies and institutions.

In the bar of the Hilton, the dancer from the Caribbean says: you will undoubtedly remember Curaçao because of a detail (Anna, whom I had met by chance a few hours earlier, had warned me that one reality did not necessarily overlap another but air stewardess between Venezuela and Aruba left her to desire). So each sentence or in the casino (what happened next made a woman say: it is late) when eyes drawn I went from table to table. Only the women were placing bets.

From instinct and from memory, I try to reconstruct nothing. From memory, I broach a subject. And that cannot be from childhood. Only from ecstasy, from a fall, from words. Or from the body differently. Emergency cell like body at its ultimate, without its knowledge, the tongue will tell it.

When Florence Dérive entered the Hôtel de l'Institut, Montréal, 1980 on rue Saint-Denis. Snatches of sentences inside. At the registration desk. It was night. Since Finnegans Wake. It was night. Itinerant, Florence Dérive such a woman. Brain — — — — — memory. The night, numbers and letters.

Florence Dérive sometimes repeats a certain number of gestures that continue to exist as writing and each time she dis/places ardour and meaning. Now, Florence Dérive is recasting her text in a bar at the corner of Seventeenth Avenue and Forty-Second Street. She momentarily abandons herself to the necessity of being what is called, among the inks, a character. Her lecture is ready. Tomorrow, Montreal.

To run over/text, I feel its effects. In order to describe precisely a singular reality born in complete fiction. *The White Scene* of May 16. It is only in the waters of Curaçao that the idea makes its way through me. With words, the same ones, here, I'll get ahead since writing is continuous with an identical knowledge, an instinct for dignity among what the styles think, fauve.

Florence Dérive, of mother born and an ultra-modern New York style, often spent her holidays at the seaside, in the house of her anarchist sister, sole heir of her maternal grandmother. House viewed again and again in a vertical shot by most of the surveillance helicopters which made the rounds above houses that might be sheltering bandaged men during the Vietnam war. Power. To be able to change America.

Florence Dérive, born of an ultra-communist, Austrian mother, wrote there are many women around us who think no differently. The sea, of course, has not many secrets. Then it was the shadow of a doubt so many words project: what form do they take?

John, the son of the Austrian New Yorker had married the daughter of a protestant minister. Raised in Quebec, Judith Pamela, had grown up near the border. *omme personnage, ( )an/s character, John had no notion of the novel.* Still, with his dollars, a director and unionized female proof-readers he built a lovely publishing house. For his wife — a roman(ce).

Oriana, an old friend of the family, often visited one or the other, brother, mother or sister. She would tell Florence stories about the cinema, windows, cries, fascism, the accent put on the conformist attitude.

Oriana, John's (ac)complice, watched to make sure he was a subversive son on the horizon of New York streets. The project was a difficult one to carry out but Oriana had chosen to compete with the Austrian, Jewish, communist mother in the field of identities. And John would become one day what he was, that is today, a manly son.

The hotels grow old like the certain models of a glorious architecture caught between the multinationals and dirt accumulated on the Greek columns in the lounge. There's intoxication and reasoning though as tourists. Broadway/porn/Gestalt. Florence was explaining to Oriana but a Corvette **sound traffic**, that love between anarchist, between women especially. A woman in the street turned around on the spot.

Intention and fervour do not make a text nor a woman of me. It makes the singular body which sometimes borrows correspondence from desire move in double(d) forms. Coincidence. Appearance. Each time, Florence Dérive says in the bars as in letters: 'womanal)/.

th'/I force familiar is desire so similar. I say after the text and the remark rises from the body of woman into a thinking woman. Dreaming is an accessory to writ(h)ing. An anecdotal incident that swallows the

17

grand passions. That evening, I'm most chilly in the Caribbean. Without thinking about it, I look at the sea, Dutch dolls. In broad sunlight.

Oh! the first chapter. Is it to say: sister brigand's skin and proud looking. The patriarchy shall not take place, should I state it? At the Velvet Snack Bar, Oriana, the (ac)complice, says to Florence as if it were still significant. 'You know, John worked a long time and cried a lot over his already discussed novel.'

The telephone, I get a line quite quickly.

Boulevard Saint-Germain, the Madison, waiter, elevator. Room: Flaubert, exactly at the place where it says that Paris is deserted because it is so hot — holidays at the seaside, in the house of the anarchist sister. Outside, the bars are rejuvenated as quickly as the books in bookstores. It was as if humanity outside, they would often sit in a café, humanity, watching her full of descriptions in their eyes.

I got up very early thinking it best not to die doubled like a hair on the pillow. A man's voice somewhere in the hotel was reciting a poem in a foreign language. My first impression was that he was having a discussion. I ate my breakfast. Then from one store window to another in the rue du Dragon, I got the impression. Echo: '*La Rivoluzione non è che un sentimento.*'

Their Austrian and communist mother said that as a Jew she felt she was a woman and an intellectual. On the wall, I saw a photograph of her when she was twenty. I saw on the wall a photograph of Florence and John with her grouped around a virile man. I saw memory in action. A photo of Florence and John at a demonstration. I saw their second cousin, poster-blue, Chicanos, grapes, on the wall of the house at the

18

seaside. The guest room. The immense verandah overlooking the sea, where each time on the yachts I looked at lightly-dressed women.

Florence Dérive — New York-Montréal — that evening. Dawn, alarm clock ringing: day of the lecture. Subject: women and torture. Hôtel de l'Institut, jour ensoleillé, Carré Saint-Louis. **Smoke gets in your eyes.** Patriarchal machine for making the blues. A little later in the day, Florence Dérive telephoned to Danièle Judith. In the evening, concluding her lecture: in summary, it is easy to understand that, determined by writing, they knew then how to imagine that each woman must be placed in service to a man, no matter what his rank, no matter what her sex. Silence: the audience's excited.

Hôtel de l'Institut, Sandra Artskin, a protestant who writes marvels without her mother ever disturbing her in order quite simply not to confound her with another woman *whose lightly dressed body* passed in front of the hotel. Text/I still feel it deeply the next day when from the window I am at the *herizon*.

to reconstitute would be the avowal of what could only in fiction be transformed by time. Still, there we were, the horizon, I will never be able to narrate. Here on the carpet, intertwined women. Visible. This is how I tried to understand the effect of the scene. And then without ever later having to nuance it. Imperative grammar incendiary. I think of this scene like the seaside, energy has no secret. She added: 'The instant is rough and senseless.' In relief, I tell its intensity, the vital force like a cliché: click, photo, the repercussion.

the other scene: I wait for her to come back with the book. I am waiting for the book. The book is there, between her hands, lips are ready to speak in an unexpected way.

a(1) The man's hand was placed on the woman's shoulder somewhere in the book. They were walking like a couple, interminably on stone, rue du Dragon.

a(2) The elevator is poorly lit. The man's jacket brushed against the stop button. He was looking at the floors going past right in front of him (a blonde woman was with him, watching him at shoulder level) depicted.

Full moon, Greenwich Village, John reels. The city is abolished in his eye. Life comes with fog, trace, panic, rain, you forget everything and begin again: children, minister, his novel. **Sexual harassment. Who do you think you are?** He followed the boy on the docks of the Hudson River, where among men torsos are (con)fused. Elevator, boy. **Black out.** New York.

Florence ends her lecture. Cigarettes, conversations in the foyer. At the restaurant, a very pretty woman says: the torture of women, I understand, yes but men, they/Florence Dérive with concentration in her thoughts replies that in Los Angeles there are only men and so no torture of women. *Ben's Delicatessen* never closes in people's minds.

Danièle Judith, the traffic is heavy. We speak in profile like a statement about civilization that marks a stop. '... We are lacking manuscripts since the death of the hero double(d) patriarchial.' It was absolutely in another book that she would know how to retrace when the moment came, the lines of a perfectly readable human form.

Florence Dérive, Jane Street, back in New York perhaps already writing, thinking like the women thinkers whom I saw and loved to watch ripening an idea in a salon while within them rose *particles of truth* difficult to understand and the women met in a linguistic hand to hand, body against body (con)frontation. Here and there, suffering, joy. Florence Dérive is like a woman who grasps that absolutely the question of intensities must be resolved but especially the one which, spatterings, bloats women until they lose their breath and their sense of duration.

Paris. Métro. Metro entrance. Garçon, carcan, choker, staircase. Livid. Free oneself from the code of aspects and asperities.

Since *Finnegans Wake*, the 16th of May, the whiteout of the scene. Abstraction urges, the future like reality. To see: infraction/reflection or hologram. Each time I lack space on the her/i/zon, my mouth opens, the tongue finds the opening.

The White Scene

i add: so there are two scenes. One dated the 16th of May*, the other very close to it. The book scene and the rug scene. Rivetted to each other as though held in suspense by writing, we exist in the laborious creation of desire of which we can conceive no idea. Or the Idea, everything that manages to metamorphize mental space. Sort of pre-requisite Idea in order to remember that networks exist. The white scene is a relay that persists as writing while the body dictates its clichés, closes its eyes on the mouths that open to repetition touched by fate in their own movement. Faced with what is offered: the extravagance of surfaces, transparence of the holographed scene.

---

* This morning even the entrance hall was sunny. There is a persistent smell of wood. A smell of coffee too.

Of mother born, Florence Dérive was a studious girl; of mother born, she was reborn each time between the deadly streets of the city. **At first a fist.** The father is a dangerous path. The city via its history. Florence often speaks about her mother facing humanity when humiliation cuts right into her round belly. Heel, Florence Dérive sometimes takes on the air of an hysteric after certain readings.

John rolls smoothly along the 95 in the direction of Maine. Wife* and children in tow. Chatting. Without that aspect of speech, where would be the fantasy of waves, the noise of the colonial dining rooms, the form of a shell? Without expression John rolls along quickly his bloody profile cut out like a landscape in the rising sun.

House viewed from the sea. View over the sea. Florence Dérive rests like an index of happiness that gives access to voluptuousness: far removed from the dictionary. Florence forgets her mother and the photographs which I glimpsed, where the viril father without too many muscles was showing himself freshly shaven. Another one of him too in the trenches.

John has seen only lightly dressed, plumed and helmeted men. Caught in the trap of his vision. Seduced. Stuntman plummeted in the subway of dreams (head in his hands): **my God!** The photo of a man in a photograph violently excites those who recognize themselves as deserters because he knows the deserter is lonely and manly too.

---

* Judith Pamela liked travel and languages. Flaubert was her favourite woman.

b(1) In the book somewhere, the man's hand touched the woman's neck. The man was walking like a man, his interminable smile accompanies him.

New York: *Wine and Spirits*. Florence Dérive writes: the concrete hunger of the after-sun or the improbable pain, let Aruba arrive, let the water come, matter too, at this moment I know only the body exposed in sleep.

Pages and lines of mirroring: **curse/curve** gaze glaze, every whirlwind that leads to the essenshe'll my love: Curaçao, you reread your notes, it is late — I know — there are islands above Arizona arrives in distress in a text — — — — skim over.

The strip on the screen, a strange linearity in the flight of fear. The newspaper you read before take off: bomb, gold, mentality. There are territories lying in wait for aerial memories. In the porthole, the utensils make tautological reflections: the cities surprise me again, repeatedly. Luminous, 'an image is a stop the mind makes between uncertainties.'*

In the hotel lobby, there is the receptionist, a bouncer, a chambermaid, an American tourist and two brown suitcases marked with the name Tom Zodiac, Australia. It is seven a.m., Hôtel Madison, the boulevard is deserted.

The hotel smells of verbena. It may be the fruit of my imagination but it smells good like Curaçao, Anna smelled of fiction, on her back, I am anticipating.

8, rue Brantôme**, the sky is grey. I enter the Museum. The feeling of being a clepsydra in the darkness of the room. Leaflet: 'In HOLOGRAPHY, the

---

* Djuna Barnes, *Nightwood.*
** 4, rue Beaubourg. Sunny day. Deserted morning.

principal element is the method of lighting....' A man is drinking cognac surrounded by a window. He smiles almost or naturally, future and public, that will be strategically set out in the cities. When the time had come.

There is always a hotel in my life to make me understand patriarchy. I have to describe them all in order to understand the most banal entrance hall, the tiniest maid's room, the rented room. Laudatory flow of four stars in the bosom of night.

Emotional territory in the wee hours. It's Friday, at this moment, Florence Dérive is keeping an eye on her text in grey New York, in front of her library, the tenacious face of Florence Dérive facing the previously discussed titles by several American authors. When it is finished, Florence mechanically reaches out her hand towards the coffee pot.

The next day, Quartier de l'Horloge: the holography museum. Rain, very touristy. Out in the open, in natural surroundings, although the expression had been formidable. Like a trick in fiction when the text topples over, I walk in the direction of the entrance hall.

coffee first. Quotations since the rooms booked are bursting with books. Successive forgettings. Silence, a thoughtful reflex which gives bodies back their pleasure in audacity. This pleasure in (it)self concerns terribly the work of formulation a body undertakes in regard to an other to reach agreement with a movement of thought. The pleasure in audacity is unequivocal: it is transparent. What makes it difficult is total and irrevocable consent; this transparency the body carries within itself like a personal history it relives in a decisive gesture. This gesture may be the movement of a hand toward a breast, the body or even to touch the sex directly. There is always clothing that intervenes and con/forms exactly to the tension of skins concentrating extremely. Conjugated with the lighting, the pleasure of audacity dangerously clothes the body of the other with an existenshe'll film from which arises, condensed in an image, the harmony that makes sense.

Oriana often returns from travelling at night. There is always a room waiting for her at the home of the ultra-modern communist mother. Oriana, whom the doorman recognizes, presses the Penthouse button. Elevator like a computer. In America, eros weighs heavily, torments, disappoints in other ways than by begging at Metro entrances. It strikes like a livid orphan adopted by a housewife. It persists through an intervening person 'something like that to maintain the fiction' (Roberta Victor) began at 16 as a high class call girl...: 'The need imposed by society for women to play roles, to play at comedy and losing battle in order to keep some authenticity still, are the recurrent themes — the real themes — of her history.' No. 8*
The elevator opens at the apartment. It is raining. New York. A few grapes on a ceramic platter before going to sleep. Between two operas.

b(2) The man looked straight ahead of him at his destiny on the door of the ascending elevator. The metal blurringly reflected his clothing without a face and the suitcase at his feet.

Basically, you say each time that you control yourself to stop *the words escaping you.* Fiction then foils illysybility in the sense that it always insinuates something more which forces you to imagine, to double. To come back to it again.

*Holidays at the seaside, on an island where, when the sun is setting, you would believe you were seeing Ulysses heave into sight on the horizon of the house (**rose wood**). 'And we looked across to the land of the Cyclops who dwell nigh and to the smoke and to the voice of the men and of the... goats. And when the sun*

---

* *Questions féministes. Feminist Inquiry.*

had sunk and darkness had come on, we laid us to rest upon the sea beach. * *Deck chairs make stripes on our backs and thighs. It is seven o'clock, Florence Dérive comes back from the village with mussels.*

Café, francs. Cabaret, tight black pants. The waiter is obviously cracked by the night, standing in front of me. The *couch* is not far off. The city distracts me from thought provoking writings. The city is this excess which takes hold of me like a vital exuberance and makes me juxtapose the sea to the buildings at the moment when I am trying in the allusion to the wee hours of the morning, rue de Buci, to write: j'avance, j'avance, she says to herself, toward repetition. I am making headway, she thinks very feverishly in order not to stop in front of a store window and see the mannequins chained there.

Boulevard Saint-Joseph, it's medical hour in the old private homes. Gynaecologists, pediatricians, obstetricians. C'est l'heure québécoise de la profession de foi. Danièle Judith is getting ready to read *Le Devoir.* In the street, the people are walking redundantly.

Ogunquit, Judith Pamela** looks in the book whose pages she has not finished cutting, the sea. John's fictions flourish, kneeling in the sand, building a fine castle. Somewhere in Judith Pamela a memory is at work that does not contain her childhood and yet makes her stretch her whole body toward the water. The elder fiction approaches, puts a butterfly on her

---

* Homer, *The Odyssey.*

** Judith Pamela is thirty and if John remembers (c.f. fiction) has two children. Its hard and eternal like a poet who brandishes his verse.

as fictive as a kiss discoloured by the water on the uncertain horizon.

New York. In the Austrian woman's salon, a young man quotes[*] in the middle of a conversation a beautiful poem that no one among the guests wanted to expect.

c(1) The man was holding the woman's hand in his arms. Like a couple, the man came back at each metro station, intact.

c(2) The Metro was poorly lit. From behind, the man was hiding the woman whose curled up hand was seen in his.

Nocturnal, Oriana sometimes lets herself be tempted by insomnia until dawn. Then she converses with the mother of John and Florence. So beautiful, the Austrian woman when she is lively in the morning watering her plants. In her dressing gown, she can very early, even before the sun has risen, talk about her childhood, about the war, about her father. 'In the beginning,' she says, 'when I was writing my first lectures, I always used to put a photo of my father on my work table.'

At the registration desk, credit card, signature. A green blotter. Taxi, the boulevard is deserted, a young man carries croissants in a wicker basket; he is sweating. Door: Charles de Gaulle airport. The city oscillates in the heat. The woman who is driving the taxi, looks straight in front of her, rarely into the rear view mirror, it seems to me that she aims her eye on a v(o)id with a single eye, the same one that makes the day coherent, three-dimensional and fictive.

---

[*] 'It is all noticed before it is too late.'

The White Scene

transparency of skins. Responding to certain signs, with complete fluidity, our bodies interlaced m'urged to fuse in astonishment or fascination. Literally thin film of skin for each other at the heart of radical motivation. Daylight. Such an abundance of light wea(i)thers the gaze. Eyes darken like a memory. Everything about this woman attracts me and words become rare. Imperative grammar incendiary, baroque eyes, I close them in profusion, traversed by the hypothesis that on the carpet, we have barely moved.

At the seaside, time is sand. Judith Pamela dreams about the immense verandah overlooking the horizon, where she could make silence and her thoughts converge, at that time when she and John spent their holidays in the house of their anarchist sister* whom she hasn't seen for five years.

At the *Eidelweiss* on the Main in Ogunquit, John and Judith Pamela listen to the pianist improvise on the first notes of Lili Marlene. Around them, men converse, brandishing their glasses to the refrain. Judith Pamela has the look of a young mother: those who notice her among all the men, gaze at her furtively, embarrassed as if they were seeing her again.

On the sand, dancers (of both sexes) mime the arrival of pirates on the island. The Hilton is lit up. The glassed-in elevator goes up again, two young people (of both sexes) on board. The pirate is dead. At the bar, he is born again, circumstances or chance for a word. Anna passes in front of me, a Ph.D. on her arm. **'All space in a nutshell.'**

---

* The one who lived everywhere at the same time. Who often 'crossed' the border. A deserter with her (most of them have become vegetarians and have opened small businesses on rue Duluth or in the mountains of British Columbia. At Nelson, their wives wear marxist skirts and little hand woven scarves. They have two or three very beautiful children who run bare foot around the '**natural food**' restaurants.

The spectacle. The box where there are always flowers. Full house. Oriana: golden helmet; you always imagine it heavy like the shield. **Curse/curve**/<u>toutes</u>.*

---

*   Stop father! Stop your curse!
     La vierge doit-elle se faner et pâlir pour un homme?
     Hör unser Fleh'n! Schrecklicher Gott,
     Turn her away from this crying shame,
     our sister's dishonour would fall on us!

Wotan

Did you not hear what I ordained?
J'ai exclu de votre troupe la soeur infidèle;
No more will she ride her horse through the air with you;
the virginal flower will wither,
a husband will win her womanly favours;
henceforth she'll obey her lord and master
and, seated at her hearth will ply the distaff,
she'll be the target and object of all mockery.
If her fate frightens you, then flee her who is lost!
Distance yourself, keep away from her.
One of you women who dare to stay near her
who will bravely defy me, take the side of the miserable
   wretch,
that rash woman will share her fate: that bold one must know
   it!
Now be off from here. Keep away from the rock.
Hurtig jagt mir von hinnen,
sinon c'est le désespoir qui sera votre lot ici!.

All the women

Woe! Woe! Terrible, terrible! Misery! Misery! Calamity!

A rhythm is a rhythm. Florence Dérive, seated on the immense verandah overlooking the sea, is listening to the tangos of Carlos Gardel. The voice merges with the sound of the waves. The daylight is blinding. Sweat all over the body. The cricket lets loose. Lupins, daisies, buttercups. Grasses...

In (f)act, Sandra Artskin passed in front of the Hôtel de l'Institut that day. She was carrying her manuscript, very proud of what <u>lightly dressed my mother didn't attach much importance to</u>. Later in the day, she'll meet a childhood friend. Sandra Artskin at once recognized the other woman who was listening gravely to three men talking at a table. The women looked at each other then embraced for a long time the lower part of their bodies separated by the table.

When Florence Dérive came out that morning from the Hôtel de l'Institut, she noticed a young woman who, just like herself, held a briefcase under her arm, doubtless bought at Bloomingdales, she thought at first, then she concentrated on a ·very specific idea she wanted to discuss with Danièle Judith before the lecture.

Le poème hurlait **of course a rose is always following opening the mind**. In the room at the Madison Hotel, I cry silently. Reality through the window is stunted. Taxi, a door opens. A women in high heels gets out of the car and makes her way to the lobby of the Madison. She resembles another woman to be mistaken for her as always. The poem was absolutely American written at the Madison, my black coffee this morning (anarchy, p.162 — on a suburban wall) the curtain brushing the sentence, the clouds are deserted, I know you are sitting, in the midst of bringing a cup of coffee to your lips, just brushing the poem, this morning, when her voice hailed a taxi.

The style was expressive (enough) in each of Oriana's gestures in the scene. It was when she turned her whole body three times in the scenery that the audience got impatient. At rehearsals, repeating her lines Oriana would sometimes defer the sound while her mouth gave the impression of singing. Then Oriana would twirl around until at last the song continued. In the theatre, a white panic seized the directors.

Le poème hurlait. Scream(ed). At the end of the corridor a man is waiting for the elevator.

In the waters of Curaçao, the whiteness is dazzling when you lift your head a little as if traversed by the complexity of our thoughts, the very perspective how complex they can be. Emotion seeks then to ruse with reality, fusing it to the self is a subsequent risk.

Full house. Oriana advances toward the august father. Her bosom heaves. Heard like a spell, destiny is rousing. Lightning flashes viva voce. Oriana sings, cries, complies and submits. **Curse/curtain/**success.

4, rue Beaubourg. A sunny day. I go into the Museum. A woman spreads her legs while a little girl floats in the space still linked by the cord and the lighting.

Leaving the elevator, I greeted the maid who was looking at herself in the big mirror in the lobby. I left the key at the registration desk. I walked down one boulevard, then another to the Seine. A woman sold me a post card. In the first café along my way I addressed it to myself in Montreal, in this way fixing this woman in my memory. The lovely expression of Greta Garbo.

d(1) With his hands, the man held the woman close to him. The man's whole body was trembling in order to keep the woman near him. Now the man's shoulder hid everything.

d(2) In his hands the man was holding the woman, a very small woman drawn on the table of the terrace with a knife while they were watching humanity pass by in their dead eyes.

Passport, tampon, customs, Danièle Judith is waiting for me. To reach out to the present, I listen to her attentively. Highway, the Laurentians reverse in my head going toward Montreal. In the rearview mirror, there are few cars at this hour. La fatigue s'allonge: first chapter suspended between mirror and city.

The telephone ringing (Florence Dérive arrived last night). Despite my fatigue, I think about writing. The apartment on the rue Laurier looks like so many others. Work table. Sleep between the lines. So each sentence or in the casino what followed, made a woman say: it is late when with eyes drawn, I went from table to table.

Feverishly I went walking through the streets of Montreal. Back to the apartment. The answering machine: *Je suis Claire Dérive.* The voice was beautiful, almost no accent. In the waters of Curaçao, the whiteness is dazzling and the eyes half close to dream the colours of the rainbow in the iris. I was obsessed with the voice of Claire Dérive, traversed by an emotion and I formulated hypotheses in the bar of the Hilton, Anna, an air stewardess, told me the story of her family or her childhood in Puerto Rico in a slum near an American base. She had said only her name.

36

Anna passed in front of me. The pirate of the Hilton says: you will get a few details confused and it is only then that you will remember Curaçao and the Shell. Life a user's manual, almost no accent.

We are sitting in the first row: it is easy to understand that determined by writing, they had known how then to imagine that each woman must be placed in service to a man no matter what his rank, no matter what her sex. In the lobby, we talk. Then the scene at Ben's Delicatessen. It is two a.m. The sea has no secret. Oh, the equivocation, civilization dreams or what in the idea succeeds in transforming mental space. Then the motor runs, I wait for her to come back with the promised book. The living force of the cliché: click, the embrace. Oh, the first chapter, the tension fecundating episode. I try not to reconstitute anything, I broach

PERSPECTIVE

Book One

▼

*I know that the amorous scene has already been viewed
and consumed in several of its strategies, I know that, I
know that, repeated, it determines the opening and the
vanishing point of all affirmation.*

as it happens the shadow of a doubt
enter simultaneous the entrance
(an I is lost here in work
instantly on entering the house
the work quickly exhausts me)
my presence merges with the scent of wood

the book, i noticed it at once
on the table, upside down and open
recto-verso the only virtual object
difficult to sustain Claire Dérive her cheek
she held out to me mise en abyme
recomposed then her gaze touched
my breast at that height where
the impression gathers holds

she holds her cheek in the hollow
a tension she holds out her cheek
i move. Raw feeling in the spine
for the moment it's so

was holding out to me the cheek (the light in
clothes a confusion between
text/ile and skin. The silence is dreadful
because without a screen; text/ured the cheek
exhausts me
Claire Dérive by instinct memory
so then smoothly to turn
her body toward the salon
in my hands, the briefcase to think
what follows

i sketch a gesture with my hand to
say when seeing the painting grey stele
of illusion, in perspective momentarily her back
when we leave the entrance
in front of the picture she turns around, i
am a relay the intrigue if i desire

Claire Dérive asked extra-textually if
this is now the movement of the hand
when agitated her fingers touched the book
and looked at me *feigning* pain
that effectively the stele, the canvas, livid tissue
then Claire Dérive slipped away adored back

eyes for the painting or the book
step by step in her stride
chasing my thoughts at regular intervals
'the strangest salon in America'*

Claire Dérive stretched out her arm
on the table the book/memory is
in the body the silence which feels it's
in amorous mouths anonymous
the body fire she said night
eclipsing bodies in the morning blindly
she spoke briefly of 'a fever
methodical'

---

* Djuna Barnes, *Nightwood*, p. 50.

in the clarity, ready to begin the invisible
gestures linking us, an attentive reading
pushes the bodies to act
                              /aerial posture
the appearance of a double rose in the clarity
fatally touched where knowledge passes
if the angel presents reflection in the light
burning mirror. i speak slowly
detached from the words i pronounce invisible

Claire Dérive was speaking in the distance
/the sea has no secret/a wave
repetitive as in music barely a break
in the voice a burn capable of overwhelming
of arousing this other
dimension astonishing suddenly lips in the name of
the burn
to escape from all categories denying
space itself and always fluid the moment

i no longer see her coming
body dense

source and condensed women

on soil and sill, experienced women
sign the spirit remakes the essenshe'll
courage in my breath some sentences whole
it was there two women
thunderstruck by a s/lashing reversibility

on the ground Claire Dérive
in ecstasy and exchange she
chose some lips the sea
in suspense in the shadow of thighs
intervals and access to the trembling
that comes after memory ravishes oblivion
tender on the ground and collects her breath
more and more precise

'by the successive arms of women'*
in the salon (i)dentical in profile the double clarity
i am indirectly detached from the sentence
cast off at pleasure suspended on her lips
it takes me by surprise versatile cohabits the cortex
one sunny day

ineluctable Claire Dérive approaches me
over all the surface skin thin film
the pleasure of audacity on my sex
her hand touching me like a reason
to write would become a permanent concern
ever since the time her hand was just there

---

* Djuna Barnes, *Nightwood*, p. 64.

caught in the clear morning by the clairvoyance
of skins ready to reproduce the infinite
in itself any idea motivates at seaside
in the entrance i am ceaseless

Claire Dérive thought of the wood when she
took words between her lips my tongue
which really suited her like a skin
saw to it that my body was lightly dressed
in front of her so her mouth from instinct could start
from memory, body at its ultimate which never
spares the future and reality that passes

i am lightly dressed on the ground
(e)longated in the unspeakable, legs open
the whole tongue of Claire Dérive
turns me inside out toward her as at dawn
the prestige of waters time comes next
in the mirror, baroque eyes

Claire Dérive knew how to die between
the legs of a woman 'moved out of death's way'*
in the forest traversed where emerged
a helmeted woman, in the clear morning
each time more numerous
on the way to the source Claire Dérive
so that between my legs she is flooded by joy

---

* Djuna Barnes, *Nightwood*, p. 64.

of my thoughts, helmet with a certainty
continents abound, it falls on me now
to have an idea, one single redoubled
with the self-same energy
so not to be spared
passing through oblivion forest right to the sea

even closer to the source
oval of the mirror detail intense
able to agree only on excess
the necessity Claire Dérive outlined
always in the angle of vision

i am eternal under tongue of Claire Dérive present like an illusion produces reality. i am elongated and eternal in the white morning which floods the scene, i am

Claire Dérive flooded the scene with her look. She was elongated translated in profile by her breasts. The beginning of a text of a same scene going to reproduce itself, incendiary grammar, all a/long persistent reality; energy of the instant senseless and rough she said the essenshe'll of it or the cliché so that the one woman and the other together we would prime the fiction, the text/ured hypothesis.

Claire Dérive opens me and puts down the briefcase
under the oval of the mirror the usual words
a movement of the hand very close
the face is forgotten directed to (the) salon

recto-verso a book promised backwards
and i composed in the scent of the wood
the links under tongue so that she speaks
breast fertile gathers by fits and starts shoal
synthesis initiated all along the body

while holding out the cheek brush her
though eyes swung back into shadow
simultaneous sentiment
i embrace her in perspective

the painting, traversed with complexity
Claire Dérive turns her back on our thoughts
i need an idea: to reply a coffee
the painting the method

to surprise me Claire Dérive urges me
to a few words pronounced without fever yet
'with a muscle in her heart so passionate
that she made the seventh day immediate'*
élan oh the chapter surprise coming out of the forest
without leaving a trace

daylight eclipsing on the book
the title without shadow of a doubt
i translated by number really
then came the transparency of bodies carried
as relays i also did say
women's arms the hope

---

* Djuna Barnes, *Nightwood*, p. 52.

Claire Dérive was sitting some eyes
speaks now about the book
from a new angle at intervals
why lie however it ties itself
hue and cry in her eyes America
in the respective position of the text

i listened attentively in order to catch
the water the deriv(ative) the scene could
claim on repeating the context
Oh, chapter briefly strayed on the by ways
of memory, i repeated the sounds
round her mouth, the liaisons
almost no accent the resonant fever

Claire Dérive when she comes back
toward me from across hides the oval of the mirror
earthly nights lunar orb
in the life of one sentence to an other
the position makes invisible the words
some displacements in the clarity
at the limit to touch

i upheld the vision without shadow of doubt
so disposed and ready with no going back
not to change a single word
in the clarity aura one version will have
she was before me leaning her body
fatally accomplished to the very limit
of the space between us

one sentence nearly complete
she speaks of gaps and links
cites a passage and i open up
where she wants to come to the source
oscillates each time textuelle

i was confronted parallel
'moved out of death's way' in the oval of the mirror
'with successive women's arms' on the sill
on the soil women collecting my breath
down there my body ignited
found itself dis/placed right here

Claire Dérive supports with her whole body
what she says about me
head full of mirrors alternating
our legs simultaneous in balance
without an alternative successive the waves
the embrace, still there are clothes
when Claire Dérive touches me

i held work as an alternative
still in my hand, necessary
in the arms of Claire Dérive
no utterance, the poem paradoxical
i leaned my head on the words
which madly came out, day sidereal

Claire Dérive pushes our sexes to the ultimate
encounter. Baroque eyes, clarity excessive
the pupil barely repetitive to wonder.
Is that an abstraction of Claire's body
a sense of Utopia, recognition?
Claire Dérive encounters my mouth
even more than existence its clothing of fire
the signs call for rigour in every approach

i uttered some words whose invisibility
on the skin of cheeks i signed
a time of Utopian arrest. i had
against my body abstract the sensation of the body
of Claire Dérive and i declared my feelings

time gives proof of the concrete in the margin
is (w)hole like a rough gesture that unveils
sense and appearance that denies it
from the depths of the seas and the cosmos Claire Dérive
affirms a body can abandon itself
in the abundance of abstractions, only

i put my mouth close to hers
the detail with ardour and repetition
of the cortex and waves decorating the sea
all the clichés, i love her, let her translate
my mouth, synapses spiral, in her service

Claire Dérive retraces precisely the circumference
of conditioned spaces ours
and the free zones all spiralled around
these are the musics without
there'll be neither Utopia, nor abstraction
nor any lip for bliss

i raised my body a touch from the ground
to utter a whole sentence
i had my back on the soil
feeling the text/ure of sense in being
thus lo(u)nging women come to ripen a thought
its contour, in fiction

Claire Dérive entered the forest
and dreams carried away by the vision
of time running out between her lips
she hears on her helmet the rain dancing
she goes through the forest dripping
and determined as is her mouth
Claire Dérive is in the dew
the herizon, lo(u)nging between my thighs

i really thought like a skin
which lives its raison d'être. i
stretched out to infinity repeated
and successive, a diffuse reply
traversed by the invisible woman i had become

Claire Dérive is invisible when she floods the scene with her look and she moves slowly in front of me, lightly in the white morning. Claire Dérive is the wave and the space the memory mirroring i hear like a sense in liberty

I was energy without end, the sensation of the idea, i was a woman touched by the appearance of a rose in Utopia's expression. i was this morning of May 16th, with Claire Dérive, exposed to vital abstraction

EMOTION

Book Two

▼

*Emotion is the dream every woman imagines, they will
desire it, those studious girls.*

In the circumstance gestures. Talk round the daily table. Later on. We are leaving, Danièle Judith Claire Dérive and I for the sea, to find Florence Dérive and Oriana in the big house, on an island, south of Cape Cod. There were superhighways, forest, scents, fields; we advanced over the continent toward the sea and we looked straight ahead of us. The highways took on the colour of the woods and cities we passed through. The highways made loops on the horizon and sometimes we had the impression we were not moving forward. Each of us took turns relaying the other on the way to the sea. The highway was *shadow and light* towards the end of the voyage, at twilight when we had left it for the slower roads which wound their way to the sea. Arriving at Woods Hole we had seen the boat we had to take to the island floating in front of us like a hanging light. We got out of the car to breathe in the sea, literally which presented itself to us under the senseless eyes of a group of tourists (in the masc.). We moved ahead toward the island without having to dream it. The illusion was great of breaking mist, winds and glaciers. The sea is grey and slow around the boat. We looked eagerly at all the forms the sky fabricates in front of us and we rubbed shoulders with each other as though inscriptions made to endure in space. Our surroundings were three dimensions our bodies experienced clairvoyantly to the full extent of our memories. Seeking the personal chemical formula, we looked at the sea and the island growing larger in the distance. We saw pink smoke in the incendiary sky. The island was in front of us, concrete like a milky goat announcing liberty. The sky was growing red around the island and our eyes tried in the *obscure clarity* to watch the sea and the island at the same time. We were advancing toward the island when light flashed across the bridge. We all turned instinctively toward the Polaroid a man held in his hands. Then lightning shot through the sky and the rain surprised us like a familiar substance. The wind rose and the island welcomed us at the same time as Florence and Oriana in their rain coats. The dock smells good of wood when we walk on it. The road was a canvas, as Oriana said, that we had to follow and complete in the destiny of our bodies sculpted in our sleep by the fatigue of the journey. The road hugged the sea which fishermen coveted, sitting in front of their fishing huts. The road was black without being night. Florence Dérive talks about villages as we pass them. Our shoulders were touching in the dark moving when the lights of a large house were visible and the car stops. The next day, I looked at the sea without having read the day before. There were boats in the distance but I concentrate on the sea, eyes slow. Claire Dérive in a kimono brings me a cup of coffee and I look at the sea in a senseless way as if for a first time, situated at the origin and very limit of my life. I saw the sea and I called it tenderly while the drizzle shivering on our limbs alternates our vision of the world. Then we are five at sun rise madly

to see the sea, atonally pronouncing complete sentences, abstract ones linking life and speech in the
horizontal hour. The day promised to be sunny behind what seemed to be an island in the distance but
who knows perhaps the mainland. A dawn mist *left
us in doubt* facing this territory emerging with the
day. At breakfast, there was fruit, cereal, bread, eggs
and coffee. We were seated around the table and
Claire Dérive said that to see us all here together
again meeting at the seaside, was a sign. Even though
she asserted that the word abstraction slipped its way
somewhere into her thought, she admitted for the
moment that it was difficult to establish a direct link
between the fact of being five women on the island
and the very idea of what could be an abstraction.
Oriana then began to talk about time and the weather
all the while searching for the words in French to say
how she imagined it. She said that she did not understand why, each time certain women got together, in
films for example, time seemed to stop around them
after having frozen them or changed them into pillars
of salt, loaded (with) symbols. After Danièle Judith
had interrupted her to say matriarchy, Oriana continued her description of time and chose to say that
there was no interest in imagining the eternal: 'On the
contrary it would be our loss to forget the hours.' I
wanted to say that ecstasy is a reality in itself which
makes time eternal. Claire Dérive affirmed that we
mustn't confound time out of mind, patriarchal time
and ecstasy because from this confusion were born
women suspended and immobile in space. A few
words of Florence give the impression of a family
narrative involving her and Claire, but Claire Dérive
pretended to have heard nothing and chain-linking
her sentences: 'You remember the *Trois femmes* and
all those from *Willow Spring*, you recall Pinky, Billy

and Willie, Ila and Magdalena. Didn't patriarchal time come to a stop around them merging them morbidly in madness, death and submission. The mother is everywhere when time stops, the mother full of secrets that cause anguish to girls left to themselves in the patriarchal ruins: cars, tires, elevators, subways, broken windows. The soul in ruin, the mind of man can no longer conceive itself differently except by projecting the loss of his deity onto the abstract bodies of a few women reunited in isolation, soul in ruins. There is lack of imag(in)ing in this which, although not ours, overwhelms us in the very exercise of our mental functions.' The voice of Claire Dérive rose with passion in the great panelled room. With your eyes, you would have said she circulated concretely with her whole body casting the deciding vote between forms of the sacred and profane. For the first time, as this morning in front of the sea, I was not afraid to hear the words of another woman, esprit de corps conquering the horizon. The whole house, windows open, burst into sunshine. It is noon. The sea in front of us is at the acme of light. Danièle Judith, Oriana and I have taken the car to go to the village while Florence and Claire make their way to the beach. The road we couldn't see the night before is lined with trees and very green foliage. At certain places, the trees cross branches above the road and we entered into shadow at the speed of light. Several curves. It is like this to the first village, slowing down, gardens, wild roses, billboards, **lobsters**, right to Oak Bluff. At the garage, we have to wait. Tires, rust, chrome. Two mechanics are stretched out working under a Corvette. There was a lot of noise. The radio was playing *Don't Be Cruel*. A man looking very proprietory approaches our car, looks at the flat tire, shrugs his shoulders while smiling like a politician: '**It**

won't be long girls.' I stared at him while he stated his price and Oriana agreed as in detective films, raids on bars, searches under warrant, interrogations at the station where they smile to the left and strike to the right. With heavy hammer blows one of the workers straightened out a dent in the fender of Meteor, Florence and Claire were lo(u)nging on the sand looking ahead, embarrassed to find themselves alone after so many years. Then Florence starts talking about their mother and John. Claire was listening but gives the impression of hearing nothing assailed as she was by very real girlhood memories of two studious girls growing up in the streets and institutions of New York. Florence recounted how their mother was full of projects and for her one trip didn't wait upon an other so much pleasure did she take from life in the meetings and conferences that defend the rights of **M**an and freedom of speech. Claire shrugged her shoulders, would have wanted to smile, but her lips full of salt did not move like they did in dreams really. The two sisters were lo(u)nging, backs hard on the ground, while Florence returned to her girlhood and the time John pushed between them for a photograph, the day of his entrance into the world of men, day of his Bar Mitzvah. **To take a picture**: John's marriage to Judith, the reception at Stanstead on the green lawn as in *Blow Up*, the chink of glasses raised while he placed his mouth on the bride's lips and while Claire, in the company of two hippies who loaded the cameras again and again like lunatics, took endless photos arrogantly and insistently. Memories abound: a lot of the Hilton in the memory of the Dérive sisters. *The tide was rising.* Claire closed her eyes and cried as if Florence had uttered vulgarities. Now Florence was quiet and looked at the sea. In silence, the words d(i)e capitate(d) the cities, the milk of gardens, **TO BE A GOOD GIRL**, the grey cat of winter in Colorado, the lunar orb, the women of the Order of Good Housewives at a conference in the lobby of the Hilton in L.A.. High tide. Ben's Delicatessen. The cosmetic counter at Bloomingdale's. **Promise to be a good girl.** The island reappeared. It's the head of the cape said Claire looking at Florence at hair level, standing while returning to the house, a towel around her hips, shivering up the spine it's clearly seen. We arrived from the village our arms loaded with food. No sooner said than done, Oriana and Danièle Judith made their way to the beach. Claire Dérive came to join me. She served herself a beer and sat on one of the stools with her elbows on the counter; silence, eyes certainly damp like the weather. I talked about the village and with the repeated gestures we make each day, as regular as clockwork, as complex as the thoughts which pass through us while the gestures and sometimes lapsus, the hand became fallible and it was necessary to lean or to stop, suspended, above reality and objects... I picked up the broken glass while saying that we must be careful of the pieces which must still be there invisible and cutting. Claire Dérive took another beer which she carried into our room, located at the far end of the house. She was lo(u)nging on the bed, I was sitting in front of the work table 'it's the primary source of use' I had skipped the parentheses 'of time' on a paper forgotten on the typewriter. Claire Dérive said instinctively: 'You should only quote as a last resort, forbid certain passages so that you won't repeat yourself.' I said feeling my anger rising that no passage was forbidden me and thinking in this way I could open myself up to all meanings. Leaning on her elbow, she looked at me with surprise as in bars when one directs one's gaze at the mirror behind the barmaid and suddenly perceives near one's shoulder the woman one is no longer waiting for now. Claire Dérive took risks in saying to me 'you should only quote as a last resort' although speaking to me amorously she said while affirming that the history of writings was worth lingering over in order to retrace what bodies had blindly agreed to make visible in the anonymity of the fictive fires which haunt some breasts. That's what explained the impression we sometimes had of confounding times 'it leaves us free to covet all the amorous mouths like a permanent concern and you see very well then that you write my love.' It was my turn to speak because we had made an agreement to devote ourselves an hour a day to the practice of replying. It was now up to me to go onto her terrain to find resonance for her words. Blindly, the word suggested passion, transport, I write: motivation machine and in my voice unforeseeable liaisons led me to distances I had to imagine, to foresee when necessary, until content emerges and makes sense. I confuse times because there continues to exist a vital abstraction in me which makes me tend to multiple memory. We were exhausted by this work and the afternoon changed bit by bit into slow emotions on our skins. *I opened my eyes*, it must have been six o'clock, I heard the voice of Oriana singing with all the energy of a Walkyrie. Claire Dérive was still sleeping and I look at her lightly dressed body. I was hearing the table is set and the voices of Danièle Judith and Florence Dérive speaking about the Gaspé, Ogunquit and Long Island like beaches in the conversation. We were sitting around the table. Danièle Judith was saying that matriarchy is a word from anthropology and it cannot be used in a contemporary way to exorcize patriarchy. This word could not be used either to elaborate some Utopia that would have restored women to their gender. I said, with a taste of salt in the mouth, on the subject of Utopia beginning with the word woman that Utopia was not going to ensure our insertion into reality but that a Utopian testimony on our part could stimulate in us a quality of emotion favourable for our insertion into history. Before Claire Dérive talks about abstraction, I added that we ought to socialize our energies so that we would in no way be victims or again to avoid having our wombs alone praiseworthy as mental virility able to serve afterward for the murder of thinking bodies. Oriana asks if I really believe the mother so fanatical. Yes and panic when the spirit of mental virility overwhelms her, leaving her in the shadow yet maternal and multiple, her face in close up, puffy, having lost the sense of duration, I believe that I have pronounced the word fanatic long enough for the women to be worried about me. There was silence that revolved around an image: I was struggling with an emotion so strong, as urgent as quick sand, that a sea of sand carrying me away by the heels, until the horizon was only a reflection on my golden helmet. Now Claire Dérive was speaking and it is night falling on our shoulders in the light above our thinking bodies. It was night she was talking about and why talk about Dublin when she said she didn't believe in the existence of that city. And why talk about the city when she was speaking about the night slow as a legend she was recounting without accent. There were correspondences between sleep and tenderness, between our twenty-four hours and eternity, between hours, abstraction and energy. The next day, the days flowed past at the seaside, before the horizon, on the beach, in the village; not identical these days which nonetheless resembled each other, slow, premonitory, hot. The next day was another day, this time of drizzle and high wind. Oriana proposed going to see the cristallophyllian cliffs found at the end of the island. Danièle Judith is at the wheel. The road mysterious in the fog. Pale villages loom up at the same time as the traffic signs giving their name, population and speed limit. Our shoulders were touching at each bend and the cliffs. Parking. Cardoors slamming. Wind. Men, women and children were walking around in the fog. Fathers carried one, sometimes two cameras slung over their shoulders. Some of them had a child on their shoulders, some on their chests, a new-born curled in a baby carrier. Claire Dérive was saying loudly, with their style, types like that should have made a career after the Chicago convention, Democrat and bloody. We made our way toward the cliffs. The cliffs spoke blatantly about days of rain, drizzle and fog as writings in the stone tell the past and the future scanned by the present as on a cathode screen. Before the lighthouse, memory had been transformed into a souvenir shop. **Shop-postcards.** *Won't you wear my ring around your neck* screamed the strategically positioned loud speakers. There is a little metal fence in front of the grass one foot high and two feet away from the cliff. This fence was used to prevent an accident. The tourist leaflet said a woman had fallen there one day apparently by accident. It said the woman was an astronomer. It was written because apparently at the time there had been no metal enclosure **FENCE**. We looked at the sea all vague **AROUND YOUR NECK** without knowing if it was the horizon. The cliffs were very tempting and fate hovered. There are islands above Arizona. There are metamorphic rocks and strata. There is stone. 'The Polis, the City of Men is a totality whose body is stone' Florence Dérive quoted from memory. There is stone.

So it was like this in the heart of the island, stone and water, slate and chalk. There are master masters, canvases and artisans. There are laborious cameras and working hands. There are sculpted, white *mujeres*, legs broken, famous fragments. There were women in the rough stone and the stone 'cut by servitude and shadows.' There is speaking stone, rain stones. There are stones pierced and resonant. There are cliffs and the city of opaque stone. There was in the heart of the stone a woman saying me millenary translucid, graven in Utopian stone. In the last resort, I thought of what Claire Dérive, my love, said about all the quoted sentences and I looked at them Oriana holding firmly on to the arm of Claire Dérive, beautiful and helmeted women from the back I saw them like an emotion which was going to produce once more in my soul this taste for the intemporal. From within this fiction Claire Dérive turned toward me, having understood that no passage was forbidden me, approached me and I had her hand on my cheek thinking to understand in this way that a text is a text and that it is as difficult to sustain as a cheek tendered. The car was moving; at certain places the foliage above us was lit up like an electric current. We were five women in a small American car who were speeding along in slow motion on a road lined with large trees during a storm. South of Cape Cod five women were crossing an island from the cliffs to the beaches. These were women who had read a lot of books and who all lived in big cities; women made to endure in time, sea, city and love. Border crossers, radical city dwellers, lesbians, today electric day, their energy took on form like electricity through the structure of matter itself. Yesterday at the origin, their energy had been made evident only in their properties of attraction or repulsion. Now in the lunar orb, they had gone ahead of the science of energy. It was five lesbians close to myths and the mainland and each one had survived in profile in the abstraction. Today a white light made them real. Oriana calls attention to the beauty of the house when you reach Cats Corner. Then all tired out each woman will go to lie down for a siesta woven with Alpha waves until the approximate hour for supper. We were sitting around the table. Claire Dérive said: at the source of each emotion, there is an abstraction whose effect is the emotion but whose consequences derive from the fixity of the gaze and ideas. Each abstraction is a potential form in mental space. And when the abstraction takes shape, it inscribes itself radically as enigma and affirmation. Resorting to abstraction is a necessity for the woman who, tempted by existence, invents the project of going beyond routine daily anecdotes and the memories of Utopia she meets each time she uses language. I was tempted one day to conquer reality, to make it plausible. First by insinuation, slipping a few words in slantwise: in order to grasp reality by the skin of the folds, in its dark holes as in a version without end, I fabricated for it a knowledge within my understanding. Danièle Judith said 'like an author' gathers her understandings one day for the books to come or for a single one, in her head, set under a different light. When you speak about Dublin and I try to understand the concept of matriarchy, is there a possible link that could suggest the thought of a work or of a consciousness at work among the images? Is it the lighting, the object or the thought by which we cause them to be born that allows us to be together here in the image of a suggestion with a (re)doubled meaning? Rainy day, the next day we read all day (time is accelerating) amplifying things from the real as if to relieve us of/with a few fictions or to begin speaking again. Those days, the sea, the island and the mainland disappeared. *We were reading*. I write around Curaçao, head tilted slightly in order to decide about one detail, then another, very worthy at the heart of a suffering that was not mine in sentences I prolong, body happy in the waters of Curaçao, plunged in my thoughts, turned towards the shore and the Hilton or else facing the horizon. Rainy day, it happened that unlike the others I was so full of energy and arrogance that I was going to take refuge in my room in order to find the form of my desire, formulas, ideas, fiction, responding only to the invading thought of inscribing the contexts and atmosphere favourable for renewing the effect produced by this vitality I was feeling. Lively into the fictional waters. Shoreless waters. Sometimes Claire Dérive came to join me like a temptation in this universe. I loved her and wisdom was abundant on our surfaces, surrounding me, entwining me, *I* became a foreign conquest then which I had to remember so as to broach the reality that presented itself to me, full of ideas in front of the dictionary recto-verso, spine broken. *Rainy day*, prose, a way of surrounding the self. Or about language among the hours which slip away, pleasure. Silence in the big house while we were reading. Then a few rare words, aerial voices in the half-light, the books are closed, arms stretch out and the whole body follows in a sigh after having been held for a long moment in a position made for reading. We were seated around the table. Oriana was <u>telling stories during the war</u>, nuancing the words deserter, subversive, revolutionary, virile in order to linger longer over the genres conformist and anarchist. Oriana was very young when her mother; she had known many theatrical men before; Oriana had grown up surrounded by her aunts who; she had sung for the first time in a; she had not wanted a child because; Oriana Longavi was her real name although; she preferred German operas for reasons of excess and adolescent dreams; Oriana took long walks in the streets of Florence between her bearded father and her mother dressed in a polka dot dress; Oriana had been in love with a girl of eight when she was five; she had felt herself dying on the operating table after having; she Oriana Longavi had been the flag bearer in the first row on a particular Sunday in a large parade nazionale; Oriana had been married to a French engineer from Bordeaux who had remarried a young Italian girl of eighteen; Oriana had learned to read *The Divine Comedy*. Claire and Florence were lovingly watching her tell these stories for the hundredth time. But for Danièle and me it was another story. Listening to her, it was in images of Saturday nights at the Élysée or at the Verdi, Visconti, Fellini, Antonioni, l'indépendence du Québec, Pink Floyd. It was Montréal Paesano, Vito, Saint-Léonard, un parti pris viril et fougeux, spark in the powder, History while women of pure gold vegetated in the mystic suburb. Subjectivities were interpellating each other in this way throughout *toute une nuit chaude de juillet* slowly. Tomorrow is another day and sunny. A rhythm is a rhythm. From the beach we heard the tangos of Carlos Gardel to which Florence Dérive was listening seated on the immense verandah her face expressive as in a distant era. In the cafés and *clandestinos* 'an entire fierce world that owes nothing to anybody, who comes there with mad hope and despair, distresses and passions that sometimes set these nights on fire'*; later, the women were called Lola la Petisa, Maria la Tero, la Mondonguito, la China

---

* *Le Tango de Buenos Aires*, Éditions J.C. Lattès, p. 31.

Benececia and Madame Yvonne. Women's names living as though in boarding schools; the most expensive room was called Los Angelitos 'above the bed, the crucifix, some religious images, some plaster medals are there as if to underline that the faith will be maintained.'* Lupins, lupanards, brothels, buttercups, the island was visible today. Florence Dérive thought: I am responsible for Utopia in my very desire spoken word in the sense of thought, where it is directed toward pleasure and has not become burdened with a malaise. I lean toward the beaches and shores to leave traces there, accepting before the sea, the fierce fire that ravages troubles and transforms the language suffering from a single version, the tongue that causes de/lirium. The missing tongue, fallible like the hand sometimes made strange in certain cultural gestures, a cut in the meaning or a hands on. Florence Dérive was listening to the tangos; the music flowed, moving alongside the path which led to the beach where we were, in the water right up to the neck, bodies floating their gazes mirroring en abyme abysmal in the dazzling whiteness of the summer light. Claire Dérive's body was close to mine and soft, legs on the alert because laughing in these moments can make mouths founder, intertwined couples, concerned with rhythm. Florence Dérive was coming down the path to join us. Agile, lightly dressed, a briefcase stuck against her hip. *La porteña* in me saw quotations in the briefcase as she 'saw in the tango the description of the picturesque part of her city, the painting of her passions, her desires.'** I was looking at Florence Dérive like an author and that evoked in

* *Le Tango de Buenos Aires*, p. 32.
** *Le Tango de Buenos Aires*, p. 45.

me desire for her like a sonorous liaison enabling the m'urging of two words and jouissance. Everything was instantaneous, une suite logique* of passages memorized to the point that they appear one, immediate and *thus* in the sensation of the body, a suite of sonorous effects arousing in me a taste for synthesis on the mouth of Florence Dérive who was seated on the sand in a way that made writing easy, briefcase placed on her knees, right on the scar. This cicatrice looks like a knot, on the knee girlhood surfaces again, braids in the morning, the ones we will undo in the evening and in the night the head invaded by dreams. I was rereading on Florence Dérive's knee, meniscus converging, the text like a knot knowing that knots may be undone in the head without untangling a plot and it was precisely about that I was thinking when searching for the solution with my eyes, I turned toward the sea. Later in the same day, it was seven o'clock, Florence Dérive came back from the village with mussels. We were seated around the table. There was wine, bread, mussels; flowers, a lace tablecloth. The atmosphere was emotional you could see it on the faces and you could imagine it in the bodies. Oriana opened a third bottle of wine when the pitch rose and we mounted the echelons in our enthusiasm, words tumbling after each other like phenomena, flash in the pan, sizzling irreversibly until a sentence of Danièle Judith encounters another of Claire Dérive and they criss-cross. 'The hunters' hatred' — 'Let's say that humanity is normal and we can inscribe intentions in the successive mater(ial) of our élans.'** The

---

* *Une suite logique* is the title of a collection of poems published by Brossard in 1970. It means literally a 'logical sequence'.
** *Élans* means both a burst of feeling in which sense it is regularly used in English and a moose, important here in the context of hunting.

hatred of the hunters and the hunger, however, which made that rough sketch of a man in the Gaspé forest say 'père'. All the bars where Danièle pursued her father among the bowling machines, the Labatts and the vomittings of the patriarchal clan installed in the taverns, lounges or sitting on a case of twenty-fours in the woods, far from everything and close to the beasts free and afflicted by the bullets of a 22. Danièle Judith, at that age, did not know about men whose History passed through the vigorous arms of her father when he brought her back towards her pregnant mother cross-like in the patient winter of bitterness. I had against me the skin of despair in my father's cabin when we were going hunting. Brilliant with anger and frost when winter approached and the season of potatoes was beginning in our everyday tin bowls. Statiscally static in front of my father who was clinging to the window's edge to recuperate when the wife of Ti-Pierre came in to say to my father that she wanted her cord of wood for noon. Danièle swore on everything in the room, swearing to death on the past, the men and the family seated around a table. Emotion, the past, faces. How can a text writ(h)e itself around a face, beloved, hated though it may be, no matter what its features, the attraction or repulsion it arouses? How can a body enter into contact with the reality of a text in order to be sparing with fiction? The illusion of bodies deluding themselves in abstraction. In January, it took a lot of ruses to survive in front of the river, ice mirror scintillating. Islet-sur-mer. Danièle Judith bit her lips. Claire Dérive looked at me, broke in on me with her volatile air. I raised my empty glass, I caught sight of myself and held out my hand toward the bottle as if to change chapters, called suddenly by the ellipses in what Florence Dérive was saying to us on the subject of New York beginning with the

82

writing in the subway. So that's what it was that, even in the heart of the island, was working away subterranean, millenary and subliminal. For the whole life you will remember the graffiti in the subway, my only daughter, expiatory prototype in the verticality of cities: invent then the essential in yourself who later as initials is going to come, work your embers into a hologram, it's the eyes' solution. 'Watchman, what of the night?'[*] is the most beautiful chapter said Claire Dérive, 'Witchman, watch of your night'[**], and I said that no form was accessible anywhere except in the outdated conformism of the dictionary such a moving marginality that answers from the interior as one answers instinctively for one self. Oriana wanted to take the floor to speak, insatiable breast in the works, breath fighting sleep lethargy of her character in the scene. Oriana is talking and the languages get tangled in the excitement; French and English; she slips in entire sentences in Italian, a quotation in german. She was all genders at once in one language or another. Danièle Judith stretched out her hand with precision towards the bottle of wine, her blue, blue eyes, all the more so since the tears this evening gave her the airs of an angel and that sent me back to my school books, to the first days of October, hunched over my desk, artist's little hand at work. *Los Angelitas,* the girls who write in boarding schools, pubic signs, clair-obscure, on the knees in penitence, the girls who write their reason, their instinctive revolt on the plaster medals. Danièle Judith was watching me speak and drink and lean over in the direction of the shoulders of Florence who was laughing 'anything might happen from the height of the cliffs.' Claire

[*]   Djuna Barnes, *Nightwood,* p. 78.
[**] James Joyce, *Finnegans Wake.*

Dérive had gotten up to go look for another bottle I was calling for while saying to her that the provinces of Ireland were five in number and Dublin must exist somewhere, full of hierarchitectitiptoploftical(e) circulation and that Dérive was a name you had to know how to live up to beyond any question of family. Claire came back with the wine, beside herself, saying **bitch, dyke,** feeling American to the tip of her nose, ultra-modern New York style. **Stop it, Michèle, watch it,** said Florence very worked up while I knew I wanted to real-ize the celebrated synthesis of water and fire that burns the tongue. **I know**, that synthesis of the double origin betrays me, **I knew, I know.** Snatches of sentence. We heard the sound of waves. It was a perfect night. It was night: shot through with tenderness, monsters and heroic exploits. It was night 'travelling through the sky enveloped in a dark veil, on a chariot harnessed to four black horses with the procession of her daughters, the Furies, the Parquae.'* As in Ireland, night would have twenty-four hours and like eternity would correspond to our dream. It's night in the sentence. In cr(y)sis, sinister and bloody patriarchy. To dislodge and deluge. Cliff. Without a global vision, we will be drowned in the flood of sons seeking their father in a direct line, fathers abstract in the desert. Thirst. Pères et fils **dismissed**, ghosts wandering among the magical, fascinating and proud bodies they have generated. All-purpose machines, **machine gun**, thinking machismo. The desert is vast filled with pyramids and the Hilton which a white light causes to rise. A form is on the look out for emotion, story. Keep a close eye on the structure and the mater(ial) reserved for it. A form is lying in wait. Thought by refraction or diffraction. At the other end

* *Dictionnaire des symboles.*

of the night, I was going to open a bottle. The cities were converging in our glasses. Women were emerging from everywhere, architecture; the sum(ma) of laws revolving in their eyes, the speed of life, the forms they are preparing to take on: numbers, grasses, books, letters, spiral, first snow. First of all in our glasses, glimmer. Each city was a document abounding in arrows. The arrows crossed the cities from end to end; some went and lost themselves in zones known but distant, barely touched by civilization, except by the arrows themselves travelling above the trees or into clearings. In the cities, the arrows were furrowing space in every sense, subliminal. What we saw converging in our glasses, that night, parfaite et claire, was an abstract and conclusive form which allowed us to glimpse, but very distinctly, how the mind of **M**an was able to conceive himself only in the form of an arrow, scarlet, in the dark mists of time; right over the body of women to put their minds to sleep: arrow-man. The cities were converging one by one, called forth by the flashing intuition we had passing through the history of art, aerial sagittarians en route to transformation, to their disintegration. Episodes and anxieties, vacant lots. The cities, lunar orb, **black out**, we needed to tame energy in order to avoid the installation in our limbs and especially in our gazes, of a mortal immobility able to make one believe in renunciation. In our glasses, a flash opening the horizon under our eyes, our very bodies in a state of thought, in firing position, mental anticipation, the arrow in the water of the soul, we were advancing calmly through the deserted streets. And we met the one who bore the name Pyrrha, disguised as a woman, as a ruse. We followed him to the letter on his heels. A night club whose neons blink out PANDORE. We went into the club. The man disguised

85

as a woman was telling another man the story of a woman who had been his mother. The story was sutured with white threads. His mother was in the image of a goddess, said the invincible disguised as a woman, but she had bad breath when she spoke. Disguised, the man could manifestly speak only of a fictive mother or by confusing gender. I mumbled into my glass: disguised but not travestied. Because the project of this man was of another order. His life, his capital(e) won out over all the games. His stake on the l*i*ne: terror. This man in front of us was the bearer of a subliminal lie generator of murderous passion slaughtering women. All women were touched; but only daughters confounded with the verticality of skyscrapers were rarely mortally wounded because the arrows were shot at them so as to disfigure them. In order to do this, an arrow was ricochetted off their bellies and while the only daughter was bending to receive the blow, the ricochetting arrow in question came and skinned alive profile and expression. Hitting the throat directly an arrow would enter *at the speed of darkness*. Every woman was struck: those who survived the rain of arrows picked themselves up again but several among them had doubts about reality forever. To deceive was the ruse and the verb took advantage of this to bring about closure in any fiction able to lose it. The man comfortably spread his legs apart, virile and deserter, anonymous and terrifying because nothing is more anguishing for the mind than to grasp that there is some information in the gesture, clothing or gaze that suddenly transforms the other into an imposter. Fear and panic install themselves in the body cheated. All reality condenses into abstraction. Doubles, splits, swindles, difficult reference. Difficult after. The haunting memory of Man, sort of sick frequency carried into the brains, along the semantic line on one side, absolute frequency of patriarchal subjectivity stretched like a net gathering all thoughts in order to unite them in a single will to power. The history of Man is so made that men have breasts which give them an advantage: when they stoop to take an interest in humanity, you can see their teeth. We are looking at Man capable of any scenario, versatile image, kaleidoscopic. The image was blurry, risked changing at each instant. Difficult to grasp. Scenarios, disguises, characters: everything of his referred back to fiction. The man comfortably spread his legs. Oriana who knew more than we did about the special effects and techniques of diversion, approached him, wanting to have a closer look. When she came back toward us, her voice hesitated, appeared incoherent an instant, then: there are plastic breasts and when he speaks, you hear a crackling as if it were a recording. He was talking about fire saying: **'I speak because I am dead. I speak because I want to reply to words.'*** I didn't hear the rest. The lighting stayed the same while the city began its noise. Men came in, drank, talked and went out again. Some of them had an accent. The room crackled. An electric current passed through the plastic beauty. Around us, as if sculpted in pain, men were standing immobile, right hand on a breast. At the speed of light and without translation possible irony of writing, a man cries out:'Night now! Tell me, tell me, tell me, elm! Night, night! telmetel of stem or stone. Beside the rivering waters of, hitherandthithering waters of. Night!'** Come l'éternité, night was opening on the horizon. The surroundings are dimensions which our bodies experience clairvoyantly to

---

* Jean Daive, translated in *New Directions*, 41 (1980), p. 116.
** James Joyce, *Finnegans Wake*, p. 216.

the full extent of our memories. The sky was growing red around the island. The next day begins while dawn alternates us in a vision of the world. At sun rise, we were five women madly seeing the origin of bodies going into the city, there where writing surfaces again, condenses itself, solution of waters, sweat beading on our foreheads. All night long exploring in broad daylight the dictionary, the context in which ideas were formed then renewed, identical and **machine gun** for repetition in our mouths beginning with the worst, *a* of deprivation. Studious girls, we will divert the course of fiction, dragging with us words turn and turn about, igneous spiral, **picture theory** an existence in these terms while the crepuscular bodies, we walk in the direction of the boat, surrounded by tourists. An expression can be read straight on our faces: tending to abstraction is an issue. Virtual rupture in the rhythm/fauna abyssal, celestial body. The cortex seeks to understand the nature of sentences

THOUGHT

Book Three

▼

Thought is without comparison to the body what the body is to the speed of light for the letter.

The glass cities were extinct. Last day on the island, I was already 'in the waters of Curaçao' in the city, caught by this tension which urges me into the present. Michèle Vallée, book three, rue Laurier. **(MOTHER SICK — STAYING IN NEW YORK — WILL WRITE — LOVE — CLAIRE.)** First tango, Anna Livia Plurabelle, the man sitting in the corridor, *la vie en prose**, did culture fit me like a glove into texture, into the screen into existence or was it going to preserve me in con/text?

---

* Yolande Villemaire, *La vie en prose* (Life in Prose).

The issue exit; the mail, parcel. *Metro*, Derive, Press, New York, 1979. Time screens books. Coffee. Alone, silence. 'To write, he said, p. 17, let us think about that.' To fill up the kettle, empty the coffee pot, wipe it. Mater(ial) everywhere. The language one never knows well enough, to be able to cite; stairs, work table. Everything will converge precisely. The sentence, initials. Integral copy. To double, reality condenses. **(MOTHER DIED — STAYING IN NEW YORK — JE T'AIME — CLAIRE.)** December the snow.

*

My private Life is a spherical map of influences and meeting points, it turns around language as a hypothesis and filters the fictive and theoretical of everyday life. In the conquest, I scent out a mental space that will not be occupied with descriptions, an anecdote here, a 'natural' inclination there to remake the same (museum, bungalow, Hilton); tendance à faire la femme (sic): the urban radicals discern in blue-prints, the favourable opportunity for intervening, dreamy and aerial.

Every image hides subliminal, formal fire, or (O liquid) accessory skull anchored at the bottom of the sea with no secret. Text which desires its characters, reality. Only language will say it: when December the snow. Claire Dérive floods a coffin with her tears, the water falls provides for the everyday finish of the Austrian mother whose lustre/sobs of her daughters.

On Fifth Avenue, elbows knock arms hard. Electric passers-by pile the jewellers at the edge of cliffs. Metaphoric rocks — — — — *mujeres* Utopia *bianca*, beautiful gloved arms, shop windows, glass. **Buildings**. (tu traces l'horizon, un détail, let's say: I should like to defend night like a thesis at the seaside)

.

From one detail, the entire continent, Arizona, the islands, Denver, indecency is simply very technical, with a finger on the map showing Curaçao and Aruba, with this gesture hiding beaches and refineries. Body and bathing suits, ties lined up on Fifth Avenue, briefcase under the arm, one goes down town, right down, on both sides. Métro, dérive flic cop fictive fuzzy, double issue (**nobody saw it**) la féminité:

Subjugated, rue Laurier, undermine the trajectory (**she's mine** Michèle Vallée in urban territory to get to the bottom of the question of monologues, raison d'être of the project: on her table, the lighting served as reference. Time flows like information in optical fibre and the mental body of Michèle Vallée hugged the shore), lays bare the expression.

Words were flying in all directions. With a view to one sense, furrowing space, a question remained in suspense: the origin over which M.V. brooded for hours on end. Meaning was in view, amplifying reality like a comet of sound (towards the source, a helmeted woman). Shattering of the museum. Thousands of fragments fall upon my shoulders. Material everywhere, pièces d'identité: notes, **lipstick**, mirror, condom, keys, money, a thousand fragments gather under your eyes in the museum, in the book, you must see them coming.

Perspective: metaphysical photos or about the singular interior, all knowledge braided, global feminine working on architecture, time, I/her force familiar in becoming. Identity in the trajectory of the body, a condensation of inscriptions: celebrates the her/i/zon.

Anna was dressed in a scarlet gown, very low cut. Earrings, dark red lipstick. She moved the doll with curious eyes in broad sunlight. Her life was a novel of love and adventure. She had just lost a month's salary on a green casino carpet. The man appeared. The heel of the man was in a state of decomposition. Those days, I am shivering in fever.

Cosmos osmosis cosmos annul, alive, a-v(o)id, gravitate, gravid, l'affame la mère la femme la femme: (**human mind**) — — — — lap/ensée th/ought. lèformes chuc chotte chatte. thforms whis per cat, mur mur lemur. The imagination always works like this, tempted by the impossible, overflowing with utopia, utter, dutter, metaphysical K.O. Fists clenched: birth babel babble. The sea has no secret, hold it tight against the retina, at the cliff. Aerial. December the snow. Visible for once; view-seable, vie-cible, life-aimable, life-target. The words function indefinitely (vanishing of the individual) as far as the eye can see in every sense: chats pitres, chap iters, pitiful cats. Piteously.

Wounds and exalted jouissance, complex affirmation of the enigmatic civilization that obsesses M.V. (is hope fanatic?) lover of musics in harmony/mirror looms/an illuminated woman, inspired and in delerium navigating the night was approaching so near that she understood the entwining of the famous braids over which the human dream had so slaved.

The cortège of bodies dancing at night the procession of girls like creative activity: our legs alternating, entwined in equilibrium, simultaneous *Premier tango à Montréal*. Tango x 4. Lovhers/(w)rite: tireless borne alive. For me, women's perfume, other tangos will outlive. Outside it is snowing on the entire expanse of language.

Alone, silence. Utopia has not stopped shining this morning through the thought I had for each word. I was writing 'it is she' as one knows for a longtime the form taken by our hands when they touch softly, precisely, eternally imprinted this score which dazzles through the instant, whose each note fills the space of the nautilus in the nebula, spiralled — — — — a woman's sex is mathematical. Geo mater.

Le divan: the books repeat us no matter the cities, they take the form of our postures. Love, sleep or arguments in the conversations. Burned by cigarettes, alcohol or pleasures — — — — the books are written by Phyrra, pirate or Albator travelling through patriarchal time the books frame the television set, let's say during the programmes for children. No matter what the difference in schedule. Solar system. The books inflame.

Real characters? The explanation hidden (research) liquid vowels. Not that I prefer to insist on Private Life but it's at the origin all the same — intimate character of complicity linked to the power of being able to be. The confidential savour between bodies tried by urgency or patience. The chalk of a character without author. Verb? Time changing. W(h)eather to(o). The horizon wounded, broken in its logical sequence. The horizon is at work said a little girl to her mother so that she would write the sentence in her grown up's notebook.

Tango, city ———— style, the city surrounded itself in a strange light. Some fog mixed with an unbearable lightness. M.V. was renewing her thoughts. Encircling the intention for the brilliant burst of things and feeling. No respite, I am moving forward, she said to herself. Infallibl(y) silence when the hand shakes. For all sorts of reasons.

Winter. Using language and the dictionary to go beyond. The imaginary, what's that all about? To invent it's necessary to be without any scruples and M.V. asserted that no passage whatsoever was forbidden her, each time abandoning herself to the cycles of vitality, to the most difficult allegiances, the ones which place equilibrium in peril and which paradoxically present a subject point-blank in the mirror.

In the waters of Curaçao ————— the necessary turbulence of the character like a web, a text/ure of sound. The narrative, this conviction which lays out complete sentences or the vigilant and everyday approach to the reality dis/played. To write, to apply oneself to words on the temples/tu longes le fragment, tu cherches ta spirale mon amour, Claire Dérive wrote from New York, in French in the text/going without saying to elaborate.

SCREEN SKIN

M.V. Knew *little of pain*; she had always put a screen between 'real feelings' and sensation. Suffering had no hold on her; each time it might unexpectedly arrive, suffering was dissipated by the effect words would produce just thinking about them. A complex rhythm was established measured in language and suffering lost itself there. Sometimes the words stayed in place (no slippage) filtering the suffering making no concession until there remained only a vague memory of it that, following its metamorphosis, took the form of pleasure, even of desire. Écran de sélection. **When you have a room of your own, you still have the privilege to screen off a corner of the room. Sparkling words behind the screen.** Draught-screen/double density; questions, gestures ————— the body commands, its will intrigues: you think. You invent a climate, a beach or a winter. Curaçao, Montréal under the lee of night, a detail with repercussions. In the concreteness of writing, abstraction continues. **Space, ink skin** by de/sign un/bossom ardour encounters proof on the surface of skin, sense, To pass through the screen with the indisputable passion we have for declarations when it's

moist, saliva and salt. Often the sex (fem.) its promise
of exploding under a streaming mouth which thinks
with the same trembling as the body in this way
renews its hope: FEMME/SKIN/TRAJECTOIRE. Dome
of knowledge and helixes. **SPIN. Take a look from
my window**, it's six o'clock, in December, dark and
headlights; the fog is only visible at the Stop — — —
SCREAM: here the mouths open on the dream, see to
it that imagination passes through the women's
temples, keep an eye out so they have eyes piercing
the dark, screen. All the regions of the brain,
panorama: cities were converging (arrow-man with
the heel in a state of decomposition. screamed in the
metro: Times, 12 point, pr(o)inted at... it was a perfect
scream) in the glass, it was the state of keeping watch
and numerous signs were coming to the surface. The
human voice had whispered 'warmly' in the ear of
M.V. that power spread suffering like whitewash (but
obliquely) on the bodies visibly distant suffering became objective like playing a role on the screen. The
human voice spoke of trials and experiences. Behind
the gleaming glass of the city, there were perceptible
forms of a state of mind favourable to suffering and
the crushing of flesh. The voice mutilated and human
passed through the glass, having a right to chapter in
the streets, hotels, parlours and parliaments. Falling
star above the islands of the arid zone, Joyce or
Dublin, the human voice blew on hair, wigs,
smoothed hair, eyebrows armpits and sexes so as to
show the architectural skin of heads, faces and
bodies. **Skyscraper**: here, the voice carried and
breached the very echo of the sirens. The mouth,
urban volcanic, cried out so loudly, that the voice
behind the glass was wearing out. Feeling was con-
suming M.V., her back (on the sand, some dances,
bronzed body, the glass elevator in the Hilton has

broken down at the third floor). Fill up the kettle, wipe the counter, touch the lumbar area (dreaming about this radical back on the white carpet in the entrance hall). **SKIN-SPIN.** The project of thought opened up sensations, made emotions recede (**back stage**). So M.V. risked finding herself without (a) character again, briskly carried away in a cosmic whirlwind and culturally vaulted at a moment in history when everything that could be thought was written as *post* or in the form of *neoliteralism*. Let's say that for the moment M.V. had no other choice but to satiate her impressions in reality itself (which would later give her an unsuspected vigour). For the moment, memory is in view like a site: all the regions of the brain. In accord with what she called a semantic fluctuation, M.V. never ran out of words. Writing is always virtual. A certain weight, obsessional and allied to a strange process of excitation which doubles utterances, intrigues the body's flesh transfixed by the event. La voix humaine (**from my window**) the morning slanted (drifting snow whiteout) slowly blocked reality, obliged M.V. to bite singularly into the landscape so that the original sensation of the meaning would well up. 'More than a simple text.' Simply a text, at the limits of the self, over the years: decent like a mobile above one's childhood bed in the heart of Montreal or artifice of fiction on the shelves of a suburban municipal library. It was book after book of sentiment stuck to the tongue (the body follows when in winter the curious tongue adventures onto metal, touching it, the tongue was caught and the body panics) about the tender tongue. Skin artful at climates: repetition, rehearsal, divan, the Hiltons, the metro, a dress cut low. Woman's breast. The voice pierces the screen. **SCREAM-SKEIN** (écheveau, decamp, détale, détail(le) Daedalus O political): ink

114

and voice meet. Here the mouth is one (lips form a single (i)dentical space; it's a dimension of silence while M.V. dreams) surface to survey so as to understand what's happening elsewhere, in the utopian head that thinks, her helmet placed on the work table: the hemisphere scintillates. La voix humaine: **SKY-WRITING.** The vision is aerial or it will not be. Because the instant calls for fluidity as a current of energy transforms reality into 'an astral hymn.' Cliffs. Meteorites in the text. Overture. Was not M.V. seeking to pass beyond all atmospheres, all climates, all sense in the stone. She was seeking to sunder what was nowhere visibl(y) written in the stone and yet which made sense and flamboyant sense in the red of (id)entities, infra p. 149. So that's what she was seeking in the heart of the aerial letter, that phosphorescence in the night like a permanent feminine presence taking on relief in stone. The image is fluid. Words lapidary. Sense troubled. All reality is condensed in abstraction. Double fluid still, a succession of images visibly of women (without chronological order) three-dimensional, make a proposition.*
SCREAM-SKIN-SCREEN rue Laurier, hunter's skull: great urban prey galloping while the human voice carries the sirens' echo off into the distance. Standing backlit M.V. looks at the snow whiteout/screen. From her window, she could have cried out and what is not writ(h)ing would have slowly dissipated. M.V. knew *little of pain* and because of this she rarely agreed to speech. Tireless her body 'in the waters of Curaçao' emitted the same desire 'the whiteness is dazzling.' Rue Laurier: **SKIMMING THROUGH A NOVEL**, me promener fièvreusement dans les rues de Montréal.

---

* *A proposition is a picture of reality,* Wittgenstein.

The voice was beautiful. Almost no accent. The present like a self portrait on the occasion of inversion: the oval of the mirror, 'senseless' work on the sense of meaning to the point of exhaustion or, until a breach of law is committed, the glass stays and that arouses memory, kaleidoscopic, convergence of the eyes may sometimes reduce to silence. **(FLIGHT 743 — FRIDAY — 10:15 A.M. — JE T'AIME — CLAIRE.)**

The road is snowy, slippery. Dangerous. Full of am-
biguities. All reflection ———— the sea, the Dutch
dolls. In broad sunlight, I drive to the airport.
Resonant blade of airplanes in the fierce blue cold
(from my window, white, abstraction, hyper-real
street) painting, I arrive, the Hilton at the bend. Park
the car. Wait. The beautiful face of Claire Dérive the
dreamer. I look in the rear view mirror at the road
covered. The herizon is at work.

Montreal in the circuit of abbreviated sentences. The human voice biographical (a tone of voice) intonation, intention of desire: it is reflected. Holographed bodies in the entrance hall. We enter. On the living room table, some typed sheets. **Is it your manuscript?**

The 'narrating' of events, of feeling, of emotion. Transparencies in the penumbra of the cortex. The shad(ow) of the mother: knot/throat. The whole family gathered together. Encircled the mother's bed. A young man was reading a poem aloud. **Skip-distance. It is obvious that she was a woman, isn't it, Michèle?**

Oui, Sarah, this abstract mother, this studious woman who, during her life, had no other motivation than to be in becoming a concrete and documented woman. Doctorial, learned and tormented, turning page after page a life without résumé, always exposed to dispersion through the ideological currents of her time.

Sarah Dérive Stein in her first dress bought in America. Flowered. A husband profiled in the photo. Metro/terrorised. Clandestine. The American dream. **Ultra modern style**, surrounded by young poets (masc.). An entire dictionary of phantasms, psychedelic couch, idyllic. Cycle of enchantment: always Schumann, resonant ground and motivation, very early in the morning, breakfast, at work in her dressing gown. **Yes, she was a woman, wasn't she?**

Since the death of her mother, Claire Dérive Stein had metamorphised herself into a studious woman; she spent every afternoon at the Bibliothèque Nationale (the smell of books, wood, filing cards). **I need proofs that she was a woman. I need to know.** The past scintillates enough to cause fear. What passes through the head at those moments overturns the subjectivity, order, ethics we have given ourselves. On that, the books say nothing/nothing on the subject of women who have become woman, busy all their lives defending with all their being the rights of **M**an.

Claire Dérive Stein, let me speak: to let some story enter my life is the most difficult thing for me. Still I work on it really. I link history to what surrounds me: it is always somewhere else. Archivist or poet on the frontiers of fiction, you will feel, even if all the memory in the world came back to you, your body flinch before the anachronisms, for ever and ever you will doubt the reality of books if rashly you look for woman in them. Yes, Sarah Dérive Stein was a woman and you carry her with you in your personal notes.

Snow. Five o'clock. Neons. **Topless.** Telephone booth at a street corner. Claire Dérive sinks into the abyss of Montreal daily life, lighting and signs. Sun dial. The sea has no secret. Pandore. At each step, the heel. Ice. Equilibrium, rhythm. A history of style in the gait.

Her sweater is lying beside the bed. M.V. speaks to her softly, tells about her Saturday night insomnias, that is to say, those which always preceded black-lettered Sunday, day of expiation in crinolines. Then, Claire Dérive leaned with her whole body on mine. Her hands are a source of warmth on the nape of my neck. The pillow has just fallen on the rug. A detail. I remember it as if remembering a week day. Daily and lovhers. No character(s).

I am writing little about Curaçao. Like a cliché, the presence of Claire Dérive stops me. Music, volume. How to escape the ordinary? Cell of urgency body at its ultimate. Indispensable trajectory: to unfold the real itself the space activated by holographic mater(ial). Force of gravity. Habiter rue Laurier dans les bras de Claire Dérive, lightly dressed, thinking of writing.

SCREEN SKIN TOO

M.V. knew little *of emotion* except that its motion could stop time and leave her suspended and immobile in space like a woman fatally stricken. But *of emotion*, M.V. knew also the inner mechanisms that organize thoughts. But — — — — — — to founder drops an emotion, cliff fragile porcelaine that emotion cannot break. Screen/translucid: matter shining and polished in vivid colours presented like M.V. an opening in the form of a crack in her life. Emotion could at any moment whatsoever come from there, to put it in another way, and take on the form of an uprising, that is to say, a collective sense. Sometimes, emotion was in this body which has a predilection for and cultivates sensations a sort of spatial equation that excites M.V. to the pitch. Seen from this angle, the screen was becoming a lithophany of changing appearance and M.V. had to begin breathing again to describe the impression she was feeling when the word *emotion* was written mechanically to follow through on the idea, sort of prerequisite, the idea in order to remember there exist dissimulated networks just like the white scene of May 16th when the idea came to me 'in the waters of Curaçao.' Emotion (**back**

stage) M.V. had a feeling of concrete certainty (when on the keys of the typewriter, **back-space**), perhaps the key to what constitutes this other dimension of desire: continu ous abstraction. Cliff, desert, the city on computer was becoming cosmic continuity: Hilton — — — — — — — — ◁ when at the feet of the cliff, emotion closed like a shell. The tiniest slit. The Slit made one day that motivated M.V. in each of the surfaces she explored with the sensation of finding her lost pains again in the blue horizon of metaphors, where the Sphinx reigns. Caught in the stone of fright, M.V. was ready to become the bust of the woman with the tempestuous head who would frighten the stranger when seeing her appearing, he would feel his pulse weaken. Pulsion, pulsion, drive, pulverizing the ink well, **I smell ashes in the ink**. Enigma/sandals/scandal of time. Oh, patriarchal memory that made people believe the Sphinx could be conquered by a man whose heels exceeded sandals. On the back of the canvas/**SCREEN SCREAM**. From thought to emotion, *he* had stayed at blue and perceived only the apparition of the enigma. **SCREAM.** La chasse à l'élan. Hunters' hatred in the Valley of Kings, the Valley of Monkeys. The desert is vast on the look out for. **Monument Valley.** M.V. knows little of emotion and does not cry over it much. Only the enigma linked to emotion matters to her and she must imagine it — that is how emotion irrigates her — to think about solving it in her tempestuous head before making use of it around the pyramids, on the boulevards, in the metro, the elevators. She carries the enigma within her, in reality: EN-SOF. Thirst for the slope in the valley of women's raison d'être oh the enigma that in obscure and ambiguous terms has for a long time kept on its face the foundation of an expression: here lies the echo. Echo struck by the sound of her name in stone, by Hera, condemned never to speak first, rat she says, ras she says, raz she says, at the first tide, the tiniest crack, Echo forbidden with no other sound but the last sound, emotion — **SCREAM** — the infernal machine dictates **WALK TALK** the tiniest crack **DIVE DYKE** volcanic echo, my future generation, from inside all my surfaces. Reflection. M.V. has entered the process of infinite emotion the one, so they say, that inverts order and arouses vertigo under the tongue each time women come there for a dénouement: to solve the enigma, bring to term the intrigue of patriarchal double meaning whose contradictory messages clearly indicate that it is a question of one way. So mental space had been reduced to its simplest expression: death. **Brain washed/human mind.** The oblique nerve, trace of sentences. Sphygmogram. History invented from scraps: continuous paper. Le tissu des vies. **Web of lies — — wedding.** Paper/paravent/screen. Did M.V. risk confounding emotion with her subject on paper (theoretically) warned as she was that the fictional cannot bear characters to be isolated, questioning first the mental space women occupy, that surrounds them. However, what the obelisks hide must be understood. All those texts whose thought had been interpolated by thousands of years of patriarchal life. Sensitized paper for printing, paper-myths of masculine legitimation. From instinct and memory, I try to reconstitute nothing. From memory, I broach my subject. It was night: blotting paper, green casino carpet, Anna Gravidas was standing a few feet from the bar, surrounded by men in their fifties, greying temples and impeccable jackets. Cigarette smoke rose like tension. To place a bet, you had to bend your bosom just a little. Two women were betting, separated from each other, from the lower part of their bodies, by the table. **Skin-screen.** The air of a tango streamed over the shoulders of the players. The casino was going to close soon. It is late. **All space in a nutshell**, sur la plage, des traces de talons, in the distance, the wounded horizon. The pirate was on board his yacht still visible, on the point of falling asleep, the motor turned off, at the pleasure of the waves. This morning of night without sleep, body in the sea I was engaged in a face to face confrontation with the sun: such an abundance of light disintegrates the gaze. **Skin-sky**: in the water, I was like a woman author filled with intuitions and signs. Against my abstract body I had the sensation that the horizon would always be accessible to me. An energy dwelt in the water of the sea on my shoulders in the appearance of water, I was the one who writes made visible in the lapsus. Skin of synthesis. Over by the Hilton, it was shining like a mirror and I couldn't distinguish the elevator or the passengers in the glass cage. **Sky-writing**: the blue horizon with metaphors without punctuation white letters blurred then and dissipated — eyes questioning the sky, mad with doubt. M.V.: 'From my window, I hear the thud of the city, I am ready to quote in order not to confuse the sky of Curaçao with the episode of the snow (**from my window**).' Because it is written in book Three that thought and writing form a single body, if the body agrees to seek permanently for its space of integrity, the volume. M.V. near her text saw all its dimensions: lines, surface, volume. (8, rue de Brantôme, l'éclairage.) A white light animated the text, justified the presence of M.V. in the waters of Curaçao 'when she lifted her head, traversed by the complexity of her thoughts, the very perspective that women abandon themselves to the idea.' Emotion seeks then to ruse with reality, fusing it with the self

134

like a whiteness dazzling reality. Then the voice became singular from one book to another, the voice broaching reality in order to surprise it in movement like a form attentive to its environment. The least fault line in the stone, borne alive by the echo, I could immobilize myself for hours, irradiant. Sphinx: double risk for mental continuity, from the continent of women to thought of consequence. The word inscribes the contribution begun again eternally from the silence in the eyes, I know it, staying with a text at the corner of a street, **from my window**, attentive to the episode of resonant buildings with slow mirrors. The city traced in the folds of continuous paper bringing back emotion.

Utopian, against my abstract body I have the sensation of Claire Dérive's body and I articulate some emotions in the room, rue Laurier, I remember having thought of writing at a precise moment. Outside, people pass alternately on the sidewalks. Above the mirror, their equivocal movements evoke some creature in the shadow. The street will be deserted tomorrow Sunday frozen solid with the cold. Claire Dérive rarely agreed to speak of the past.

It's Sarah who taught me to read. During the time when she was madly in love with Cecilia. Cecilia spent long hours at the house. She came in the afternoon. Sometimes for an evening when she was officially invited by my father. Florence and I listened in on all their conversations all the while pretending to play. It happened they would retire into my parents' room for work which required much concentration.

....

Sarah Dérive Stein had wakened her daughters to tell them about the magnificent evening she had just spent with Cecilia. *Persephone* danced in the room 'no stranger could call her theirs.' Persephone danced in the eyes of Claire and Florence listening to their mother like music confronting dance, wheat and hell.

The room is big. A brown abstract dresser when you enter the room. Photos, numerous and ancient. On the bedside table, a carafe of water, a handkerchief. At the foot of the bed, worn pink slippers. A young man is sitting on the edge of the bed, chest tight, as if suspended above Sarah Dérive Stein. Standing, John stays at her side. Their heels move closer in the half-light. Florence and Claire, at the foot of the bed, look at their mother. In the doorway, Oriana Longavie and Judith Pamela stand motionless.

Rue Saint-Denis. Red light. Danièle Judith and Claire Dérive are talking in profile in their winter coat. A girl comes out of Sex-tup. A man too who puts a hand on her collar. She talks loudly. More loudly. He takes her hands with one hand and speaks in the noise of the traffic. A young man straightens up and turns toward John. The two men watch each other cry, fixedly. Oriana moves into the room. Her breast touches Florence's back, her right arm is around Claire's shoulders. Judith Pamela reads again in her thoughts a patient letter from Sarah Dérive Stein. Complete suspension of movement.

A complex rhythm was established measured in language and suffering lost itself there. Hôtel de l'Institut, rue Malines, rue Cherrier. Red light. Claire Dérive would walk in the absolute cold to rue Laurier. December, snow. M.V. was outside looking at the passers-by each one more future than the next and at the image of Claire Dérive who at last, visible at Stop, raised the collar of her coat among the cars' headlights. In the entrance hall, you had to take off the *tuque*, scarf, coat and gloves, very lovingly. This face.

The metro was crowded. A smell of wet wool increased the feeling of being cramped. M.V. condensed her thought at each station. Lighting. Uncomfortable bodies miming the cold in the glass doors of the subway car. M.V. was standing straight among the shoulders. Derive Press had just published the book Florence called *Mind and Wind*. In the letter which accompanied the package, Florence spoke of mental space and of representation. 'How precious to me were the days spent at the seaside. New York is in a bad state. Oriana is on tour. I send you kisses my lively sisters. Florence.' The waiter passes over with a cloth, takes away the two glasses, the stained table cloth. Takes the order.

Tango, texte ————— la ville. No matter which cities, books repeat us, take the form of our emotions. The necessity for certain positions prior to feminist thought. Yes this body takes up a strategic stand in the streets of the Polis of men, yes, this body dis/places the horizon of thought, if it wants, this body is generic.

Claire Dérive's voice has no accent. Tonight, she is the one who will speak the thought of our bodies recalled and called forth like figures exposed to the light. Il neige, rue Laurier, our arms are crossed in such a way that the words we utter resonate from inside our breasts. Symbols suface again on our pellucid skins that reveal them. This night, our eyes disclose the plan of cities. Concentrated in the pectoral area, the generic body prepares to breathe words.

SCREEN SKIN UTOPIA

By beginning with the word woman in connection with Utopia, M.V. had chosen to concentrate on an abstraction of which she had an inkling. From the moment when M.V. had used the generic body as expression, I knew that behind her the screen would be lowered and she would be projected into my universe.

She would have no other choice but to agree. *Agree* is visibly the only verb that can allow verisimilitude here, the transparency of utopian silk/self (in my universe, Utopia would be a fiction from which would be born the generic body of the thinking woman). I would not have to make another woman be born from a first woman. I would have in mind only the idea that she might be the woman through whom everything could happen. In writing it, I would have everything for imagining an abstract woman who would slip into my text, carrying the fiction so far that from afar, this woman participant in words, must be seen coming, virtual to infinity, form-elle in every dimension of understanding, method and memory. I would not have to invent her in the fiction. The fiction would be the finishing line of the thought. The precise term.

————————————————————

Itinerant and so much a woman. Brain ————— memory. Night, numbers and letters. At the ultimate equation. I would loom into view.

Time becomes process in the ultra-violet. I am the thought of a woman who embodies me and whom I think integral. **SKIN (UTOPIA)** gesture is going to come. Gravitate serial and engrave the banks with suspended islands. I shall then be tempted by reality like a verbal vision which alternates my senses while another woman conquers the horizon at work.

Utopia <u>integral woman</u>

Gesture is going to come: a sign I'd trace, a letter that would reflect me in two different voices I would be radically thinking like a ray of light, irrigating the root, absolute reality. The generic body would become the expression of woman and woman would have wings above all, she'd make (a) sign. Plunged into the centre of the city, I would dream of raising my eyes. FEMME SKIN TRAJECTOIRE. *Donna lesbiana* dome of knowledge and helix, already I'd have entered into a spiral and my being of air aerial urban would reproduce itself in the glass city like an origin. I'd see this manifestly formal woman then inscribe reality, ecosystem.

From there, I'd begin, the woman in me like a centre of attraction. Surely life if life has a term death would be another, concentrated like a neuron, still it would normally be a sign. I am on the side of life if I die *in* slow motion, I occupy space in Utopia. **I can push death away like a mother and a future**. Brilliancy, amazement today that energy the lively affirmation of mental territory is a space at the turning point of cosmic breasts. J'ÉVOQUE. JE CERTIFIE MON ESPOIR. **SKIN** utopia slow vertigo. I work on the context of the already written of our bodies' fluorescence, I perform the rite and temptation of certainty so that it ramifies. I would see a formal woman opening up to sense because I know that each image of woman is vital in the thinking organism — — — — gyno-cortex. At the end of patriarchal night the body anticipates on the horizon I have in front of me on the screen of skin, mine, whose resonance endures in what weaves the text/ure t/issue the light when under my mouth the reason of the world streams down. M.V. agreed. In her eyes, it was epidermic this will for serial circulation of spatial gestures which the letter had initiated. **Skin**.

The mother came back sometimes without knowledge of words, to tell everything and also that it would be for a last time, asserting as a hypothesis that she would give up her right to speak to M.V. whom I had never so much watched writing what she felt straightening up her body in front of the Sphinx, invested by the enigma word by word progressing (on her face, in slow motion, everything from the fiction became visible in each cell and la peau travaille **skin I win the double glory of** ses seins sont miens et grammatrice **look at the double you** of the state we formulate fair tide in the city. **My *m*ind is a *w*oman**.

It wasn't possible then to lose sight of hope in the hologram over what had never been a detail. In the waters of Curaçao, Anna Gravidas swam with long movements her arms alternating in the water. Sitting on a deck chair, I saw a head come out of the sea, distracted and lost rediscovered rising out of the waves: the sun was wiping out the anecdotal cards of the casino. To like one's project, repeat it, fuse with it, cite it Claire Dérive had said one day at the seaside. I should die of shame for having heard only the word citation.

The dictionary was lying beside the bed, Recto-verso. Hundreds of definitions. Who defines? I lean over to pick it up. It weighs heavily at arms' length sort of agitated animal. A the impression. The hyper-realism of words transforms the body/the body unfolds D N A. The long spiral dissolves time. Each second is no more than an image. I open the book. Sequence of the instant: sidereal day. I see her coming. Between the minute when she entered the Hôtel de l'Institut and the one when the woman came out, undoubtedly that night she focused on the very precise idea of the verb define which led her to question all definitions concerning women. Continuous surface, waves come in relays, is said also about sensations and sentiments.

She said wave it's a matter of an ordered sequence of terms sitting in the middle of the room in the however of real things. At arms' length: body/dictionary. The circuit of abbreviated sentences. Cortex spiral. The woman utters some invisible words 'it's reality point blank' or hackneyed words at the same place to break off suddenly. Short-circuiting emotion, idea, concept. Hope according to the curve of crystalline lens; from where I draw on the (f)actuality of words.

At grips with the book, baroquing. Sweat beads. Resort to the window to track down sonorities, poetry passes through the millennial quotidian in order to come back to the idea of her I have been following well beyond my natural inclination, she who pre-oc-cupied thought has seen words come like foreseeable attacks and changed their course. She is the one who inhabits me and who familiarizes me with the universe. Scintillates in me. All the subjectivity in the world.

Utopia shines in my eyes. Langu age is feverish like a polysemic resource. The point of no return for all amorous affirmation is reached. I am there where 'the magical appearance' begins, the coherence of wor(l)ds, perforated by invisible spirals that quicken it. I slip outside the place named carried away by the thought of a woman converging. Anatomical slice of the imaginary: to be cut off from linear cities to undertake my dream in duration, helmetted, virtual like the woman who gathers up her understandings for a book.

M.V. had straightened herself up, slowly turned her head her gaze caught between the window ledge and the horizon. Le poème hurlait **opening the mind**

Nicole Brossard

Hologram

*Translated from the French
by Barbara Godard*

Guernica / A Novel

Hologram

Prose Series 7

Nicole Brossard

Hologram

*Translated from the French
by Barbara Godard*

Guernica

Montreal, 2011

Original title:
Hologramme

Hologramme was first published in 1982 by Éditions Nouvelle Optique
and a revised edition was published in 1989 by Éditions de l'Hexagone.

Printed in Canada.
Typeset by Megatexte, Montreal.

Antonio D'Alfonso, publisher and editor.
Guernica Editions Inc.
P.O. Box 633, Station N.D.G.
Montreal (Quebec), Canada H4A 3R1,
The Publisher and the Translator gratefully acknowledge the financial
support from The Canada Council and
Le ministère des Affaires culturelles du Québec.
Legal Deposit - 3rd Quarter.
Bibliothèque nationale du Québec and National Library of Canada.

Language is a spectacle of what we cannot think as such (women).

Preface

The ordinary is a circular bas-relief filled with unspeakable motifs. The ordinary lays a hold upon language for its profit Oh four stars merge the names of streets gynaecology duty. Ordinarily the man holds the woman in his stuntman's arms lifts her up carries her off, metro elevator parking lot, make her read what he wants. The ordinary puts posters up on walls, crosses them out, takes them down the ordinary dis/places itself artfully from city to city you carry off with you in the taxi rusty rolling which drops the passenger at the foot of a suburban wall — — anarchy p. 34. The ordinary dreams only with muscle: words of the heart. The ordinary watches humanity pass by like a dream in its café sculpts her or lays low, leans hard on memory. The ordinerve is repeated in the courageous trenches behind its gas mask. The ordinary doesn't escape me. Yes, a user's manual.

*what distinguishes itself by nothing in particular
amazes me as a style. Florence Dérive says in bars or
in books: 'womanal)/. But how does the expression* as
it affects her come to formulate* the 'nnameable will it
be current praxis. I would not know how to narrate
what is hidden in language but to see clearly in it yes
the lightning flash opening up the horizon to a thinking perspective. The part of pleasure inscribed in
language is the one that amazes at the very moment
when pleasure converges. At the turning of a word,
the brilliance of a woman who makes sense: image
quivering with the whole body. Reality condenses in
abstraction, the skin works, acoustic relief, I hear the
'nnameable without knowledge of the words I
pronounce: I see her coming. The nature of sentences
is limitless visual information running over our
bodies at the speed of light. It's the embrace, then
when women are separated, virtual again let's
reconstitute the original woman from aerial roots.*

---

* 'Following a rule is a *practice* and *therefore* one cannot follow a
rule "privately".'

idea: remember that networks exist. A three-dimensional motif (I see her coming body blurred dance) she came near me in the casino shoulder close alla volaban angeles oscuros - y angeles ciegos por el otro lado *like an inclination, let oneself be desired and I desired to see her coming. Blindly, the word suggested passion, the voice modulated unforeseeable sounds, runs again to the window Oh to defend night, its twenty-fourth hour without this gram of ordinary sense, in its entirety, this body — — — — born when, in the light, in the arms of Claire Dérive, noon, synapses in the contour of fiction, for life, mine on the horizon, at work.*

holos *hurlait le poème in the sharp streets of the city, on the border of language, chromatic fringe.* **Skin/link**: *yes, language could be reconstituted in three dimensions beginning with the part so-called pleasure where the lesbian body, language and energy fuse, Oh the first chapter, the book promised when she rubbed against tribade in the words of her tribe torrential* torrere *celebrated synthesis of water and fire that burns the tongue. I am burning, I am burning, solution of the eyes limitless.*

*whoever passes through the mind like a long term
memory breaks convention (when one pronounces
l'Islet-sur-mer, Long Island, Lac de Côme, Lac Echo
and some girls look at the boats passing while their
mother cries out with all her strength in their direction the table is set and in their glasses water reflects
the ordinary which is recorded, bread, melting butter,
rocking chair, screen, flies even, the reality of hands
dirtied, knees, with a single glance of the eye capable
of reflex) exposes oneself, and telescopes: to follow in a
woman's footsteps. Celescope — — I see her coming
women syn-cronous in the morning each time more
numerous, élan vital.*

theory above the cliffs like islands overhanging the desert, the reality of syn-cronous women modifies the horizon, the streets of the glass city, reflexion made, mental space for a contemporary vision. De-riv(ative) drift curves the horizon. The poem broaches the human voice. **From my window**, *des phrases en surface <u>about her</u> superpose her multiple giving a sign of life. The women are numerous in the room, women come to hear Florence Dérive. I was sitting in the first row, my briefcase on my knees. The lecture finished, the men's questions ricochetted over the lectern. Florence Dérive followed her thought even though distracted by the to-and-froing in the direction of the university discothèque. Rock, background noises, psy-k'idyllic garage, mechanical. Lots of noise. Chronic chrome. Women's discomfort when the crowd gets excited. Outside, we walk between university buildings. It is night in our coats. The snow Spinster Spiral. The contours of fiction take form in our mutual tongues. Then abruptly Florence says:* **'Sometimes, Michèle, my mouth is full of ashes as if our kingdom had been burned down forever** *indescriptible, tu comprends.' With a sign of my head, I did not want to agree.*

'At certain moments we reach limits it's limit origin ex
hausts 'story stele. In the crossing, smthg is (can)celled
where one believes grass such vertigo, verre glass
mirror image gradual lentissimo weaves the screen
horizon light era skin scream aim(e) **skin** version
where it works.' Unspeakable, I would have replied
touching her on the arm, she told me several months
later in a bar on Forty-Second Street. New York is in a
bad state. Rain. Clearly cracked by the night, the
waiter takes the order. Sleeves rolled up, tight pants,
turns round skirts around the tables, punches the
clock comes back toward us while a woman sitting at
the next table, rummages in her purse: **lipstick**,
mirror, heart on her sleeve. When we go out the rain
has stopped. Some window-dressers are redoing their
display. The naked mannequin is asleep standing up.
On Fifth Avenue, beautiful gloved arms, we take the
subway. In the first car, a man is pawing... ....., his
interminable smile. From my window, it was the
episode in which M.V. stayed stuck to public codes in
distress among the knotted signs, **string** corde raide
of the semantic line, obsession with words,
manuscripts with double meaning like a proposition
about civilization marks a pause. I know it, she
stayed with a text at a street corner.

*the angle of vision from where I am the impression
collect yourself at the limit   I enter into time (I'd
like to talk a bit about myself) of writing, where I saw
in a reverse shot like a verb rather than an other is
calculated in micro-seconds in thought so that she'll
emerge. I enter into time from the angle where words
turn so fast that (l) disappears if the ange(l) offers
itself for reflexion in the light. In the angle, however,
when in slow motion, **string**, strangles, closes up on
her like a dictionary, memory-clappers. Her breath,
her breast. **curse/curve** the feminine plural would
be used in a strange a/normal manner. I see her
coming in the ang(l)e when the sentence divides in
two; sometimes one, like the sea has no secret, the
other; coupled compatibl(y)* language runs along the
decor, defers the sound sometimes while the mouth
opens.*

---

* 'In order for the one to represent the form of the other, there
must be something that is the same in both.'

alright, so I'd like to talk about myself at the most inopportune moment, agreed poetry a woman who resembles another, agreed Sunday walk the boulevard is deserted, agreed reality (I noted only emotion, what causes it in expression) a foreign tongue 'non è che un sentimento' echo, agreed contracted in the ordinary, agreed, spoken by me about myself this book at a distance projected into my universe I saw it like a motif at the origin of my life, anterior and future, agreed I am in common cause with the utopia of the everyday.

skin tongue rises to the brain like a concept hard at
work on rumour she lo(u)nges on the sand she is
naked in the representation of time the rumour circu-
lates that she exists really the woman rises in the eyes

like a sensation in the midst of fiction abundantly she is at the image of what light(ly) pronounced offers itself to the imagination perfectly readable then skin tongue rises and surrounds her serpentine spiral from the height of the cliff she conceives herself as one names what she is in a word dis/placing oblivion she is attentive to the braided letters then skin in relief she had felt it coming in her belly the word butterfly opening its wings she had said nothing about it in the book she knew to be by a woman rumour confounded with the confidence that a man was a woman perhaps does she really think it in order to conceive in her language the mobile that would expose her between mental and the thought of the idea that a woman could be a complete resonant sentence dreaming that a source of coherent light is related to the project of seeing her come it's rumour skin language rises it's real and unreels the vertigo of seeing there

clear(ly) in her arms the invisible is a perfectly
readable woman in the version of ecstasy and duration she is contemporary her breath her whole body
for a sound sounding dream the legend drifts de-
riv(ativ)e into a poem in the exploded history the

profiles scintillate from where I am it's the contour of the real the idea profuse she is a subliminal woman come into the night of time to rest her gaze on an other woman before the war before an other conflict still the same sex torsos heels anatomical slices in the trenches the body's weapon exposed epsilon pendant peacock père knows how to make Persephone hell uterine sections childhood is reborn she is born from a phrase skin language surrounds her a woman expresses herself

in her body it's a sensation not forgotten in the
representation of space when the idea sees the day
s/lash in the brain the metaphors where the heart is
catch fire under the effect of a coherent light the ash

of letters eyes interrogate mad with doubt or other-
wise mater(ial) so that the abstract body abandons
itself to light suppose it's Claire Dérive incarnating
day this time in the form of an everyday woman like a

permanence of the mind turns the pages of the dictionary turns in the half-light from the back view in profile face (Oh no! it's 'the front part of a man's head' undermining then all anterior expression 'what is preceding, former, earlier of time' the

language will reproduce with you in the folds of skin
this endless version of your body from now on unal-
terable because I know how to move with you in the
volume *torrere* coherent light skin the sentence rises
into the eyes a projection of the self in

addition syn-crony of the page the room the city in the night numbers and letters in the name of what she is the human form came toward her visible in all morphology occupying her thought like a territory that goes without saying she

had come to the point in full fiction abundant(ly) to
re/cite herself perfectly readable

Notes

All quotations in Book One are from Djuna Barnes, *Nightwood*.

Quotations in foreign languages some of which have been translated are from Pasolini, Homer, Ashberry, Joyce, Wagner, Daive, Wittgenstein, Gonzales Tunon, Gertrude Stein.

References:

Fléouter, Claude, *Le tango de Buenos Aires*. Paris: Éditions J. Clattès, 1979.

Die Walküre. Deutsche Grammophon, Berliner Philharmoniker directed by Herbert von Karajan.

L'âge d'or du tango. Carlos Gardel. RCA.

Chansons d'un pays quel conque. Quarteto Cedron, Polydor.

In profound recognition and with thanks:

Daly, Mary. *Gyn/ecology*. Boston: Beacon Press, 1978.

Causse, Michèle. *Lesbiana*. Paris: Nouveau Commerce, 1980

Stein, Gertrude. *Tender Button*. New York: Vintage, 1962.

By the Same Author

Poetry
Aube à la saison (1965)
Mordre en sa chair (1966)
L'écho bouge beau (1968)
Suite logique (1970)
Le centre blanc (1970)
Mécanique jongleuse followed
by Masculin grammaticale (1973, 1974)
La partie pour le tout (1975)
Le centre blanc (1978)
D'arcs de cycle la dérive (1979)
Amantes (1980)
Double impression (1984)
L'aviva (1985)
Domaine d'écriture (1985)
Mauve (with Daphne Marlatt, 1985)
Character/Jeu de lettres (with Daphne Marlatt (1986)
Sous la langue/ Under Tongue (1987)
A tout regard (1989)
Installations (1989)

Prose
Un livre (1970, 1980)
Sold-out (1973, 1980)
French Kiss (1974, 1980)
Le sens apparent (1980)
Picture Theory (1982, 1989)
Le désert mauve (1987)
L'amèr ou Le chapitre effrité (1977, 1988)

▼

Theatre
L'écrivain *in* La nef des Sorcières (1976)

▼

Essays
La lettre aérienne (1985)
L'angle tramé du désir *in* La théorie, un dimanche (1988)